The Honeymoon's Over

OTHER BOOKS AND AUDIO BOOKS
BY ELIZABETH W. WATKINS:

The Bishop's Bride

The Honeymoon's Over

a novel

Elizabeth W. Watkins

Covenant Communications, Inc.

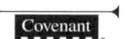

Cover photography by Picture This. www.sarastaker.com
Cover design © 2010 by Covenant Communications, Inc.

Published by Covenant Communications, Inc.
American Fork, Utah

Copyright © 2010 by Elizabeth W. Watkins
All rights reserved. No part of this book may be reproduced in any format or in any medium without the written permission of the publisher, Covenant Communications, Inc., P.O. Box 416, American Fork, UT 84003. This work is not an official publication of The Church of Jesus Christ of Latter-day Saints. The views expressed within this work are the sole responsibility of the author and do not necessarily reflect the position of The Church of Jesus Christ of Latter-day Saints, Covenant Communications, Inc., or any other entity.

This is a work of fiction. The characters, names, incidents, places, and dialogue are either products of the author's imagination, and are not to be construed as real, or are used fictitiously.

Printed in the United States of America
First Printing: April 2010

17 16 15 14 13 12 11 10   10 9 8 7 6 5 4 3 2 1

ISBN-13: 978-1-59811-946-6

To Richard

Acknowledgments

I offer my thanks to Kathryn Jenkins, Kirk Shaw, Jennie Williams, and the rest of the staff at Covenant Communications for their support and friendship. Thanks go also to Curtis Larson and Marshall Willis, two good friends and fine men who looked over parts of the manuscript and gave helpful input. I appreciate the many readers who have kindly encouraged me to tell more of the story of Andrew, Jeanette, Gina, and their friends. I hope that this work meets their expectations. And, as always, I thank my husband, Richard, for his steady confidence in my writing abilities and for suggestions that have enriched this book.

CHAPTER 1
Sweet Home

The tires hummed dreamily against the road, adding a subtly sleepy backdrop to the silence in the cab of the sedan. Andrew McCammon shifted slightly in his seat, just enough to stay awake without disturbing Jeanette as she dozed against his shoulder. He didn't want to turn on the radio and chance breaking the mood the concert had left. He had never attended a classical guitar concert before, but he could tell that this one had been something exceptional. And if such events left his bride feeling this romantic, he would be attending a lot more of them in the future. Letting his mind revert to the tender, intimate strains of Rodrigo's "Fantasia," he indulged in a long, wistful sigh. This evening's fling in "Spain"—disguised as a concert hall in Salt Lake City—had ended an all-too-brief honeymoon. Now it was back to real life—or maybe surreal life, since tomorrow morning he would be sustained as bishop. Still, he had no inclination to rebel against his fate. It was the prospect of that calling that had pushed him, a socially reclusive widower for three years, into the three-week whirlwind courtship that had resulted in his present newlywed status. In all good conscience, how could he complain about a situation that had made him so happy?

"Daisy," Jeanette said suddenly. If her voice had been any louder, Andrew might have jumped; he had been certain that she was asleep. "Daisy Fleabane. How's that for a name for this car?"

They had owned the vehicle just long enough for Andrew to get to know its idiosyncrasies. Personally, he had been leaning toward something more like Maleficent or Jezebel. But Jeanette did seem to have a knack for making the creature behave. "Well, if we've pretty well decided that it's going to be your car now, you should have first choice of names," he replied. "Are you sure you don't mind giving your car to me?"

He asked for courtesy's sake only. Once he had discovered that Jeanette's car refused to start about once every three months, it was a foregone conclusion that he would take charge of the Beastie. He would rather handle its moods himself than worry about whether Jeanette was stranded somewhere. And thanks to his previous car, Bucket of Bolts—recently retired to some obscure junkyard after that eventful morning on which he had pulled Jeanette out through its skylight and proposed marriage to her—he was accustomed to carrying around a trunk full of tools.

"I don't mind at all, if you don't," Jeanette replied drowsily. "It seems to run better for you. Maybe it needs a man's touch." She snuggled a bit closer.

As he felt for and clasped Jeanette's hand, Andrew conceded that Daisy did have a few good points, two of them being an automatic transmission and a bench seat. Turning his head slightly, he inhaled the delicate, lingering scent of her perfume, his gift to her from "Paris" earlier today in the form of a tiny but costly scent boutique near Main and Third South, touted as Les Arômes de l'Amour. The fragrance was like Jeanette herself—fresh, sweet, subtle, and altogether irresistible. He pressed a quick kiss against her hair and drove on.

All too soon, their exit loomed up ahead. Andrew gave the wheel a subtle tweak, and Daisy coasted down the ramp and stopped at the traffic light, shuddering slightly. He began mentally rehearsing how to prop the storm door open and unlock the front door of the house then turn quickly enough to pick Jeanette up and carry her over the threshold. Memories of carrying Susan, his first bride, over the threshold of their small student apartment began unfolding in his head; automatically, he shut them off. He had decided weeks ago that it would never be fair to compare the two women he loved in any way. He knew that Susan would approve of his second choice—had already approved it, actually, from beyond the bounds of mortality. He owed it to Jeanette to build with her a new set of memories as unique as the old had been, with never a word comparing the quality of the two. Anyway, comparing Susan and Jeanette would be like comparing a ruby and an emerald—both of them beautiful and precious beyond anything he deserved.

"Almost home," Jeanette observed softly, lifting her head slightly as they rounded the last corner.

For a second, Daisy's headlights illuminated the front of the house, bringing the front porch and door into sharp relief. Andrew stiffened with shock. "I don't believe it!" he almost shouted. Jeanette's head jerked up sharply.

Parked in front of the house was a patrol car. And knocking on the storm door was the chief of police.

"Chief Ridley?" breathed Jeanette. "At this hour?"

Instantly, Andrew put the lid on his temper, which was threatening to boil over. Chief Ridley had made himself the ever-present bane of Andrew's existence throughout his hasty courtship of Jeanette. Frustrating though it was to see the chief on hand yet again to interrupt this long-desired romantic moment, it wasn't likely that he would have chosen to do so at ten forty-five on a Saturday night unless there was a compelling reason.

As if reading Andrew's thoughts, Jeanette exclaimed, "An accident? Not one of the kids!"

Pulling into the driveway, Andrew braked and switched off the engine simultaneously. Daisy sputtered indignantly and died in a series of tremors and hiccups as both front doors flew open.

"Chief? What's going on?" called Andrew.

The chief skipped the three steps completely and landed on the sidewalk. "Mr. McCammon! Thank Go—oodness! We've been at our wits' end. How fast can you get to the hospital?"

"Who is it?" gasped Jeanette.

"Tiffany. She's been asking for you for hours."

Andrew stopped midstride. He didn't have a daughter, daughter-in-law, or granddaughter named Tiffany. In fact, he wasn't sure he knew a Tiffany at all. "Who?" he asked blankly.

"Tiffany, for Go—osh sakes! My oldest girl! She got in a wreck today and can't move her legs—can't feel anything from her waist down. She says you're her house teacher or something. Needs a prayer from you."

"A blessing?"

"Yeah, and I couldn't find the other guy she asked for, either—Lafe Olson, the name was. Rick Farr's out of town, and I didn't know where else to turn."

Andrew thought quickly. He was still in best dress from the concert, and the oil flask was in his suitcase. "Lead us there," he answered, turning back toward the car. Jeanette was right beside him.

Chief Ridley crossed the lawn in two bounds, calling, "Can't do that! Police escorts are illegal now. Jump in the back."

Andrew hesitated for an instant. A ride in the backseat of a police car generally meant a lot of unpleasant notoriety, whether deserved or not. That wasn't the ideal situation for a newlywed bishop. But there was an injured woman involved, and Jeanette already had the trunk lid lifted and was opening the suitcase. Chief Ridley was dancing beside the patrol car, bellowing, "C'mon! What're you waitin' for?" at the top of his voice, and the porch lights of neighbors were starting to flick on. Deciding that notoriety of some kind was inevitable, Andrew hastily located the oil flask, shut the trunk, grabbed Jeanette's hand, and ran for the patrol car. In seconds, they were leaving the subdivision with lights flashing, siren blaring, and tires squealing.

"Where are we headed, chief?" asked Andrew, grabbing an armrest as they rounded a corner to avoid toppling onto Jeanette. Hastily, he located his seat belt and clicked it shut. Apparently, having a family member in trouble was, in Chief Ridley's opinion, sufficient reason to disregard both traffic laws and the principles of physics.

"West Park Regional."

Andrew thought it best to let him concentrate on getting them all to the hospital as visitors rather than as additional casualties. Turning to Jeanette, he said softly, "Lafe's gone, and I need a companion. Do you have your cell phone?"

She had been fiddling with her seat belt clasp, but at these words she dropped it, fished her cell phone out of her purse, and turned it on.

"Try to get hold of Steve Roylance. See if he can meet us there."

Jeanette tapped the phone's small screen. "What if they're out?"

"They'll be in. It's after curfew."

Jeanette smiled slightly. "True . . . Steve? It's Jeanette. Andrew and I are headed to West Park Regional so he can give a blessing. Could you please come to assist? . . . Chief Ridley's daughter Tiffany. Andrew's her home teacher, I guess . . . Oh, *she's* Sister Barlow? The Sunbeam teacher? . . . Yes, we'll be watching for you . . . Yes, thanks—bye. He's on his way," she added, closing the phone and groping again for her seat belt clasp.

Andrew winced, not altogether from pain, as another abrupt turn slammed him into the door and turned him into a cushion for Jeanette. *Sister Barlow! This could be a tough one.* He had been assigned the Barlows mere weeks ago, following his release from the high council, and had visited them only once. Glancing ahead at the chief, he whispered to Jeanette as she finally snapped her seat belt shut, "Sister Barlow's a recent convert. She's excited about the Church but still doesn't know much—

she was really uncertain about accepting a call to 'witness to the kids,' as she put it. Her husband's a mechanic at the military base."

"Could he help with the blessing? We should have asked," Jeanette murmured back, but Andrew shook his head.

"Rhett was brought up barely active and quit church at age thirteen. He took the discussions along with his wife when she insisted on it, and he's been progressing very slowly since then, but he's still a deacon."

"They have children, don't they?"

"Two—a girl two years old and a boy born just a few months ago."

Jeanette shivered. "A crisis like this could make or break the whole family."

Andrew tilted his head toward the front seat. "Not to mention the in-laws."

"Wow," Jeanette whispered.

Andrew couldn't have agreed more. In the briefing he had received from Rick Farr, the departing bishop, the less-active Barlow parents and the Ridleys, who weren't Mormon, had figured prominently. In addition to his list of members already in need, Bishop Farr had compiled a list of people within the ward boundaries who were "on the verge," meaning that he knew the incoming bishop needed to watch them but didn't know why. Andrew was sure that he had just discovered why.

Steve Roylance pulled into the hospital's parking lot as Andrew was helping Jeanette from the backseat of the patrol car. Chief Ridley was practically bouncing with impatience. "She's on the first floor. C'mon! They were still reading the CT scan last I heard." He strode off, leaving them to scurry along behind him.

Steve took a moment to smile at the McCammons sympathetically. "That was good of him not to put you in handcuffs."

Jeanette's eyes widened. "Handcuffs?" she repeated, horrified.

"It's police policy to handcuff all backseat passengers. I suppose he was too preoccupied to remember that," Steve explained, his unconscious smile widening into a grin.

Andrew's eyes rolled heavenward, and he shook his head. *Thank goodness for that, anyway,* he thought. *Here's hoping the stake presidency has a good sense of humor, too—not to mention my new ward.*

* * *

It was all Jeanette could do to keep up with the men as they strode through the doors and entered the maze of corridors. No one challenged them; Chief Ridley's uniform probably assured that. The hallways were quiet until they entered the trauma ward; then people in scrubs seemed to be everywhere, intent on urgent errands of one kind or another. Chief Ridley barreled straight down the middle of the corridor, letting them dodge him. The others followed in his wake.

In less than a minute, they had entered a room where a plumpish, dark-haired young woman with reddened eyes lay on a gurney, strapped to a rigid, boardlike brace. She was surrounded by monitors and personnel. A lean young man with shaggy hair and two or three days' growth of beard, also with red eyes, sat beside her, gripping her hand so hard that Jeanette could see white indentations forming in it. An older woman, also plump and dark-haired but graying at the temples, hovered behind him, sobbing aloud. In the background stood a middle-aged couple, faces grim as they clung to each other and looked on silently. These people must be Tiffany, Rhett, Mrs. Ridley, and the elder Barlows, Jeanette surmised. She wondered who was watching the children.

"What's the word?" barked Chief Ridley. The hospital personnel jumped, and the Barlows flinched. Mrs. Ridley sobbed louder. Tiffany answered, her voice trembling just slightly.

"The doctor isn't back yet, Daddy. But you've brought Brother McCammon. I'll be all right once he gives me a blessing."

All eyes turned to Andrew. He withdrew the vial of oil from his pocket with his right hand. He seemed calm enough, but as Jeanette watched, his left fist clenched tightly behind his back. Furtively, she extended her arm and stroked it softly. It relaxed very slightly, and he turned to Steve. "Are you ready, Brother Roylance?" he asked, his voice steady but not quite natural.

Steve nodded silently. The medical personnel, apparently familiar with the procedure, made space near the head of the bed and retreated to the edges of the room. Mrs. Ridley, still sobbing, made her way to the chief and buried her head in his shoulder. Rhett looked something between confused and defiant, but he didn't move. Andrew squeezed in beside him and held the oil ready.

"May I have your full name, Sister Barlow?" he asked.

"Tiffany Marcellina Ridley Barlow," she replied, voice still trembling.

Andrew bowed his head and repeated the name. His voice was deep and solemn. Jeanette marveled at how soothing it was to hear him declare his authority and announce the purpose of the blessing in the familiar words. Once he had completed the standard phrasing, instead of turning the sealing of the blessing over to Steve, he continued. As she listened, his confidence seemed to grow with every word he spoke. He assured Tiffany that she was not facing this trial as a consequence of divine displeasure or neglect and that her Heavenly Father knew and loved her. Because of the purity of her heart, He was allowing her to be tested so that her faith and example could positively influence those she loved. Andrew closed by expressing the great confidence her Heavenly Father had in her ability to weather this crisis well.

Andrew's voice remained strong and steady to the end of the blessing. Jeanette reverently echoed his amen. Once Steve had, in a few words, sealed the blessing, she opened her eyes and was startled to see the perspiration that was beading Andrew's forehead. He sagged slightly, as if drained. Tiffany, on the other hand, was smiling through flowing tears.

"Did you hear that, Rhett? God *hasn't* forgotten us! He *trusts* me."

Rhett frowned. "Can you feel anything? Wiggle your toes," he demanded. Clearly, he preferred results to assurance.

Tiffany's smile faded. The bedding covering her feet remained still.

Rhett bit his lip. Tiffany's began to tremble. "Now, don't do that," she pleaded. "I'm new at this. Give me time to get my faith strong enough."

Steve cleared his throat in a lawyerlike way. "I think you have the right idea, Sister Barlow. Maybe all of us need to apply our faith to this situation." He glanced around the room. The Ridleys looked back at him, puzzlement showing in their faces. The Barlows averted their eyes. The silence became heavy, but no one broke it.

A quick step sounded at the door. "Sorry about the delay, Mrs. Hamblin," said a voice that tried to be brisk but was edged with weariness. A slender, fit man about Andrew's age entered the room and quickly scanned it as if searching for something—perhaps a progress chart. "Another patient was convulsing . . ." He trailed off as he finally looked Sister Barlow in the face. "Oh, for . . . I'm on the wrong floor. I'm very sorry, ma'am." He turned to leave, but the doorway was blocked by another professional man, taller but stoop shouldered, graying, and tired looking.

"Well, Dan, I haven't seen you in ages. What are you doing in trauma?"

"Just switched into autopilot, I guess, Gary. I should be up a floor."

The taller man entered. "Since you're here, let me show you something. I could use some advice." Stepping to a light-box attached to the wall, he shoved an X-ray negative under its clips and turned on the light. Then he unrolled a sheaf of printouts. "Look at how this compares with the CT."

Dan peered at the X-ray, then at the papers. "Mmm. Looks like a favulo-dincorum compression." At least that was what Jeanette thought he said.

"Standard procedure says to martalize the carstin. What do you say?"

Dan looked up, shocked. "No way! That's led to rastulodation in eighty percent of cases. There's a better treatment—betsilatorsion, it's called. I learned about it back East at the annual neurosurgeons' meeting."

"Have you seen it done?"

"Not in person, but they showed us three video clips. It's a tad tricky, but it frees the septulian with a minimum of damage. And the worst that can happen is that it won't work. Then the patient is no worse off, at least. Only problem is that it's got to be done within twelve hours of the trauma."

"Think you can do it?"

Dan shuffled his feet. "I don't much like to experiment," he said evasively. "That's why I switched specialties."

"I know," Gary said pleadingly. "But at least you've seen it done. I haven't. And we've got about four hours left."

"You don't have anyone out here who's ever done it?"

"I don't know. I've never heard of it before."

Dan hesitated. "Well, if you can't find anyone else, I'll give it a try."

Immediately, Gary turned to the nearest person in scrubs. "Get on the phone and contact every hospital within fifty miles—a hundred if they have a chopper pad. If there's anyone out there who's ever done a betsilatorsion, I want them here within the hour."

As the medical personnel scattered and Doctor Dan left the room to seek out his patient, Doctor Gary approached the foot of the bed. "I guess it wasn't too professional to go through all that in front of you, Mrs. Barlow. But Dan is one of the best, and if this method works, it's better than any alternative I can offer. What I'd do would have you on crutches for life, at best. He'd be giving you a chance to walk again."

Tiffany looked terrified. "But . . . but he said he's never done it before."

Gary sighed. "That's the downside, for sure. But, as he said, if it doesn't work, you'll be no worse off. And I'd sure like to send you home with working legs to chase after those two babies of yours."

The silence grew heavy again. Jeanette saw the anguish in the young mother's face and longed to comfort her, but there seemed to be nothing to say. Finally, Tiffany turned to Rhett. "Will you pray for me the whole time?" she asked.

Rhett bowed his head. "Yes," he choked.

Tiffany turned to her parents. "Will you?"

Chief Ridley began to sputter slightly, but his wife cut him off with a firmly spoken "Yes!"

Tiffany looked next at her parents-in-law. "Will you?"

Brother Barlow glanced at his wife and spoke for them both. "I dunno that our prayers are worth much, we're so rusty at it. But we'll try."

Finally, Tiffany turned to Andrew. "What do you think, Brother McCammon?"

Andrew drew a deep breath. "It seems to me that your faith is already working small miracles. There's no other reason for the right doctor to have arrived at just the right moment when he's not even supposed to have been here."

"We'll pray for you, too," Jeanette added, and Steve nodded agreement.

* * *

It took less than twenty minutes to determine that no one within a hundred miles had ever performed a batsoleration—or whatever it was. Andrew could not understand medical terminology any better than he could speak Swahili. Doctors Dan and Gary readied themselves for the procedure while a group of nurses prepared Tiffany. As they began to wheel her from the room, Rhett walked alongside, obstinately ignoring the nurses' protests, until his wife ordered him away, her voice sharp with strain. "No, you stay put! The doctors don't need to be tripping over you every time they turn around. Besides, you said you'd pray the whole time, and you can do that better in the waiting room. If you really want to help, that's how to do it." Looking hurt, Rhett let go and fell back, but Tiffany quickly added, "I love you, hon. Remember that. I'll be back soon."

Rhett bit his lip hard and turned to follow the procession of parents that Steve was leading toward the waiting room. Andrew put a reassuring hand on his shoulder and drew him along. "She's in good hands, Rhett. Let's go do our part."

As they followed the rest of the group into the waiting room, Andrew listened as Steve, with the practiced ease of a lawyer consoling distressed clients, spoke calmly and cheerily to the Ridleys and Barlows. "We've all got our marching orders, I guess." He scanned the room, which was half full, and steered the group to a mostly vacant corner. Once all were seated, he spoke more softly, just enough above a whisper, to avoid attracting attention. "Tiffany has been taught to address God as our Heavenly Father in the name of his Son, Jesus Christ, but in the present circumstances, the form is not as important as the intent." Most of his audience looked slightly puzzled. Steve clarified neatly without seeming to do so. "Whatever you say and however you say it doesn't matter as much as how sincerely you want to believe that God will hear and help you."

Troubled, Mrs. Ridley broke in. "My old minister taught me that you had to have the Spirit to be heard, and if you had the

Spirit, you'd be shouting aloud. Should I shout right here in the waiting room?"

"That isn't necessary," Andrew answered. "Remember the story of Elijah in the Bible? The priests of Baal shouted themselves hoarse all day long, but all Elijah had to do was talk to the Lord in a normal voice. He'll hear a whisper or even a thought if you direct it to Him in faith."

"So what do we say?" Chief Ridley demanded gruffly. "'Now I lay me down to sleep' won't do it, and that's the only prayer I remember."

"Well, what do you want from him?" Andrew asked.

"For Tif to get well, of course!" the chief snapped.

"Then that's what you ask. Just remember this, chief: you're addressing the Being who engineered the creation of the world and everything in it. He isn't like a waiter in a restaurant that you talk to only when you want something and complain to the manager about if he doesn't come through right away. He's someone you'd visit after you've showered, shaved, changed into your dress uniform, and shined your shoes." Andrew listened to himself with growing amazement and a little uneasiness. He wondered what he was about to say next.

The chief blinked. "Like the head inspector?"

"In a small way, I guess. The head inspector could get you into trouble if he took a disliking to you, but God isn't like that. You're His child, and He loves you, no matter what you've done. But it's tough love, and you have to earn the right to His help. He's not going to fork over blessings to someone who will use His name as a curse in the next breath, claim that everything turned out all right by sheer luck, and undermine someone else's confidence in Him. Would you give the time of day to someone who did that to you?"

A rather strained silence followed. Andrew held his breath, wondering if he had gone too far. He glanced briefly at Jeanette, who was looking anxiously at Chief Ridley.

"Well," muttered the chief at last, "I guess I wouldn't. I don't get it yet, but we promised Tif we'd pray the whole time, so we'd better get to it."

"Bowing your head and closing your eyes will help you concentrate," Steve advised. The chief did so. "Simply address God, our Heavenly Father, in the name of Jesus Christ, and explain to Him your desires, humbly and respectfully."

"And if you feel the prompting," Andrew added, "you could discuss with him what you'd be willing to give in exchange."

Chief Ridley's eyes flew open indignantly. "You mean I *bribe* Him?" he shouted in a half whisper, his voice cracking on the offending word.

"You can't bribe God," Andrew answered as reasonably as he could, resisting the impulse to roll his eyes in incredulity. "He already owns it all."

Steve cleared his throat. "I think you'd agree, chief, that a bribe is meant to solicit or reward lawless behavior. You would not, for instance, be bribing your officers and patrolmen when you recommend them for merit raises. If I'm not mistaken, that would be called an incentive for continued and effective lawful service."

Andrew gave Steve a grateful glance. The infusion of logic had bought him some time and patience. "The term we use in a gospel context is *sacrifice*. It means that we are willing to give up what the Lord most wants us to give up. Usually, that's some behavior He's already commanded us not to do." Andrew paused, fearful that the word *commanded* would hit another sore spot.

But the Ridleys had apparently heard of the Ten Commandments and didn't object to the terminology. "That's reasonable, I guess," the chief growled, "but I'd still like to hear a prayer before I try to make one up myself." Rhett and his parents nodded involuntarily.

Glancing around, Andrew saw that the other people in the waiting room were too taken up with their own concerns to notice the group in the corner. In fact, several of them looked as if they were engaged in earnest prayer themselves. "I'll demonstrate," he offered, bowing his head.

* * *

At eighteen minutes past one in the morning, a weary-looking Doctor Gary entered the waiting room and approached the group in the corner. Rhett shot to his feet, as did the police chief.

"The pressure has been relieved," the doctor announced with a tired smile. "Everything is looking good. She's in another surgery now, but before she went under the anesthesia, she moved her toes and responded to stimuli on the legs."

A collective sigh rose from the group.

"I'd advise all you good folks to go home and get a good night's rest," continued Doctor Gary. "About three thirty tomorrow, come on back. She should be awake then, and we can all discuss recuperation and therapy."

"Therapy?" blurted Rhett. "I thought you said she could move her toes."

"She can, but she's got some internal bruising and a few fractures that she couldn't feel before. The other surgical team's at work right now setting bones. When I left, they were all saying that it looked better than the X-rays had led them to believe. I'd say that she's a very fortunate young woman."

* * *

Chief Ridley dropped the McCammons off at their home just before two in the morning. Fortunately for the remains of their romantic evening, Andrew reflected glumly, the chief had continued to waive the backseat handcuff policy.

"I think you handled your first crisis as a bishop quite well," Jeanette commented as they watched him drive away.

Andrew fumbled with his key ring, trying to locate the key to Daisy's trunk. "Don't speak too soon," he cautioned. "I'm not a bishop until this afternoon sometime."

Still, he could not deny that he had felt considerable heavenly influence in the events just past. The feeling was elevating enough to help the luggage seem a bit lighter as he and Jeanette moved it from the trunk to the porch. Maybe the Lord had a special mantle for bishops-to-be, to prevent them from shooting themselves in the foot right to begin with. Maybe the mantle of a home teacher was expandable enough to suffice until the stake presidency set him apart for his new calling. However it was, he was thankful.

Exhausted though he was, he had just enough inspiration left to solve his quandary from earlier that night. As soon as he had unlocked the door, he took Jeanette's suitcase from her hand, jammed it against the open storm door, and swept her into his arms, with a long kiss to mollify any protests. "Welcome home, bonnie Jeanette," he whispered as he lifted her over the threshold.

As she relaxed against him, Andrew felt a warm sensation of soothing comfort wash over him. He was not alone anymore. Jeanette was with him. Jeanette loved him. He was a husband again. If becoming a bishop could bring this about, it couldn't be all that bad.

CHAPTER 2
The Mantle

It was done.

Andrew could not deny that he had gotten cold feet at the last moment—had looked around the stake conference congregation rather desperately, in fact, for opposing votes. There hadn't been one. The hands of the stake presidency had felt heavy on his head, and the mantle lay heavy on his shoulders as memories of all that Bishop Farr had discussed with him in their "briefing" session a few long weeks ago came back to him.

But he had no time to dwell on it now. He was at home, and his children were smothering him with thrilled congratulations. Fiona, seven months pregnant, had buried her face in his chest, while her husband, Spencer, nearly shook his right arm off. Mark, with his fiancée, Alyssa, at his side, was pumping his left arm just as enthusiastically. Twins Eric and Kevin were pounding him on alternate shoulders; their wives, Sheri and Heather, kept the grandchildren at bay, awaiting their turn to mob him. In the background stood Jeanette, her silver-frosted dark hair glinting like a halo as it framed her face, her melting green eyes, and her glowing smile.

He recalled the words of Russ Newman, his stake president and Susan's cousin, as he had instructed him just before the ordination. "Lesson one: family first. You'll never be able to teach that to your priesthood holders if you aren't living it. Do whatever you need to fulfill your calling, but schedule your family time with an indelible marker. Double-schedule it, if you have to, but get it in regularly." *Sounds good to me,* he thought. *I guess the mantle can wait for an hour or so.*

Following the setting apart, he had sent his counselors and clerks home with instructions to enjoy some family time, eat a good dinner, read over the revised membership list, and meet him at the bishop's office at seven thirty that evening to begin the process of restaffing the ward. The splitting of the stake and consequent realignment of ward boundaries had played havoc with all the church units involved, but especially with the Twenty-second Ward, of which he was now the bishop. Nearly all of its current population had come from other wards. Of its former membership, only eleven households remained. Four of them contained bishopric members—including a clerk and an executive secretary—three contained less-active or part-member families, and two contained families of other faiths. Clearly, his bishopric would need a great deal of inspiration to organize a functional ward by the following Sunday.

Despite the late hour of their arrival home the previous night, Jeanette had taken the time to glaze a ham, stud it with cloves, and set it cooking in the Crock-Pot. The children had brought side dishes and dessert to supply the rest of the meal. Andrew and Jeanette had claimed that this gathering of the extended family was simply a chance to formally celebrate the impending addition of Alyssa to their number. Nevertheless, all his children's suspicions had run wild when Jeanette had invited them to attend the stake conference session as well. Andrew was grateful that the reorganization had taken place at the beginning of the meeting to put a rapid end to their speculations. At the rate they were going, they would have had him elevated to stake president, if not General Authority, by the end of the meeting.

Dinner was a merry affair, although it did cause Andrew a pang when Eileen, his oldest granddaughter, asked innocently, "Gwampa bipup now? Den who Gwampa?" As her mother,

Sheri, explained that Grandpa could be a bishop and still be her grandpa, Andrew sincerely hoped that she was right.

He felt another pang as he left the cheerful party behind for a solitary drive to the hospital. He had promised the Ridleys and Barlows that he would be present when the doctor met with Tiffany, Rhett, and their parents to hear what course her recovery should take. The brief drive gave him plenty of unwelcome opportunity to second-guess his most recent decisions.

Perhaps, Andrew fretted, he had been playing the martyr when he had insisted that Steve and his wife, Gina, not accompany him to the hospital. Gina had, after all, been the Relief Society president up until the reorganization this morning. Officially, she and the rest of the ward officers had been automatically released along with Bishop Farr, but Andrew had already received the unmistakable impression that the volatile Gina should stay on as Relief Society president. He had not told Steve about this, however, wanting to wait until both his counselors had a chance to concur with him. He winced as he imagined what the cost might be if Gina took this simple decision in the wrong way. He would have to depend on Steve to put things right.

The meeting at West Park Regional was informative. Tiffany, inspired by the restored feeling in her lower limbs, cheerfully agreed to the rigorous program of rehabilitation Doctor Gary presented. Then, just as cheerfully, she skillfully extracted commitments from husband, parents, and in-laws for everything from baby care to daily family prayer. Andrew could not help but admire the way she managed them, getting them to consent to all manner of life changes that they would never have made otherwise, all on the basis of her willingness to face any amount of pain and effort herself. How could they refuse, after all? Even Chief Ridley, after a bit of hopelessly weak resistance, consented to make time to attend her next family home evening "to help with the kids." *Tiffany's going to be our new Primary secretary*, he thought in a flash of inspiration. *Rhett can do the legwork and attend the nursery with his toddler. And his parents will have to keep the baby nearby, of course.*

Tiffany would be in the hospital for another few days, and Rhett had no leave time left from work since the birth of the baby, so Mrs. Ridley and Sister Barlow worked out a schedule to supply child care in the afternoons and evenings, when he was gone. According to his parents, Rhett, in spite of his mechanical skill with fighter jets, could barely manage a toaster. Still, Tiffany committed him to fix breakfasts every day. Sympathetic to the young father's plight, Andrew committed the ward to supply a week's worth of lunches and dinners. The families agreed to meet the following Sunday for a review and planning session for the weeks to come. *By then,* Andrew thought complacently, *Gina will be sustained, and she can come in my place.*

Andrew's first action upon emerging from the hospital was to phone home. "Jeanette? Do we have any food left from dinner? . . . That's great. I have a use for all of it . . . Yes. Wrap it up in foil, and we can walk over with it later. And let's be prepared to show Rhett how to reheat it . . . She's doing very well, but the family is going to need the ward's helping hands for a while . . . She's just been arranging everyone's lives for them, so she's worn out now, but I'll bet she'd love the company tomorrow . . . I'll let you know after the bishopric meeting tonight . . . Chocolate cream pie? You bet. I'll be home in ten minutes. See you, sweetheart."

It felt wonderful to call someone that again.

* * *

Jeanette was justifiably proud of her new family. With one accord, all of them had donated the leftovers of their ample dinner to the Barlow family. Fiona, in addition, had volunteered to visit Tiffany at the hospital at her earliest opportunity.

Andrew arrived home in time to give each of the grandchildren a hug and to trade a few jokes with his children before they left.

"Do you have time for pie before we head over to the Barlows'?" asked Jeanette, presenting a triangle of chocolate and whipped cream for his inspection.

"Absolutely," Andrew replied, seating himself at the lately emptied table. "Mmmm," he murmured through a mouthful. "Just like Su—smooth, like silk. Fiona hasn't lost her touch."

The stammer and quick recovery weren't lost on Jeanette. Immediately she turned away to pour a glass of milk to go with the pie, fighting the tiny needle of discontent that pricked her feelings. She had tried to prepare herself emotionally to bear graciously any comparisons, real or imagined, between herself and her husband's late wife, but the truth was that being compared with Susan would never be anything less than intimidating. *Andrew still loves her, and he should. He's bound to mention her now and then,* she scolded herself. *You're being hypersensitive. You didn't even make the pie—Fiona did. He's just remarking that Susan taught her well.* By the time she turned with the full glass in her hand, she had quashed the feeling and assumed a carefree smile. Andrew, on the other hand, looked distinctly embarrassed.

"I . . . uh . . . almost hate to give up that ham, it was so delicious," he confided as he took the glass of milk from her. "Thanks, dear. But the Barlows are in real need. Sister Barlow tells me that Rhett doesn't know one end of a can opener from the other."

"Hey, bishop," she teased, bending to brush a quick kiss on his cheek, "you can spare the ham. You've still got the cook."

"So I do," he agreed, catching her wrist and pressing the back of her hand to his lips. After a quick visit to deliver dinner to the Barlow household, he promised himself, he would make sure that she understood how much he appreciated that fact.

* * *

From the moment he stepped into Rhett Barlow's home, Andrew could tell that the brief visit he had intended was an impossible dream. "Thank goodness you're here, bishop!" Rhett shouted above a duet of loud wails. "Tif told me to give the baby some formula. Which formula does she mean? The ones in the cookbooks look all wrong. And how do I tell clean dishes from dirty ones? Oh, and she didn't say whether I should use dish detergent or laundry soap in the kids' baths. Do you know?"

By the time Andrew and Jeanette had helped the hapless young father feed, bathe, and clothe his children in clean pajamas and lead them in prayer—one of Tiffany's most emphatic requests—their stay had stretched to two hours and forty minutes. Andrew had to leave his new bride on the porch with nothing but the memory of a hasty kiss before racing hurriedly on to the bishopric meeting.

When Andrew entered, panting after his headlong run from home, he found Steve, with his ever-present smile, entertaining the second counselor and clerks with lawyer jokes from what seemed to be a vast collection. After greeting the bishop warmly, he concluded with a tale of a lawyer aghast at a bill presented by his plumber, giving Andrew a chance to catch his breath and gather his wits before taking charge. (". . . And the lawyer said, 'I don't even charge my clients fees this high!' So the plumber replied, 'Neither did I when I practiced law.'") Willing himself to breathe slowly as his bishopric savored the punchline, Andrew silently marveled yet again at the keen intelligence and boundless tact of this man who looked for all the world like a giant, worn-out version of Winnie-the-Pooh. It had been a fortunate day when Andrew had met him and recognized what a remarkable counselor he would make.

The meeting, filled with earnest discussion and punctuated frequently with prayers for guidance, lasted over three and a half hours. As it progressed, Andrew's experience in the high council proved invaluable, for he had met a number of his new ward members through his assignments in their wards. One of them—Ron Purser, his new second counselor—lived in the neighborhood from which over half the ward's new households came. And his membership clerk, Bruce Arrowsmith, owned and worked at a popular retail store in the town and had met many more of them. The result of their input, combined with plenty of inspiration, was unanimous agreement on all quorum and auxiliary presidents, a full staff of teachers—for the coming Sunday, at least—and several challenging but reachable ward goals.

Andrew had already scheduled one precious day off from work for this Monday immediately following his call so that he could read the bishop's handbook. However, a number of urgent welfare matters and known spiritual crises were brought forward during the meeting. These needed immediate attention and quickly ate up Andrew's planned afternoon of study. With the proverbial ox already in the mire, his bishopric agreed that half an hour or so of interviews, held during the Monday lunch hour, would be permissible for Andrew to call the quorum and auxiliary presidents. Then he would deal with these other various emergencies as best he could before ending the interviews no later than six o'clock. Brother Arrowsmith, whose work hours were flexible, volunteered to be present as well. At last the weight of the mantle Andrew wore seemed lighter.

He drove home, very tired but pleased. The coming week would be a continual round of interviews, he knew, but the task had begun to seem possible. Yet as he pulled into the driveway and let the Beastie roll to a halt, he was disappointed that no light seemed visible behind the blinds of the living room. His mood became more subdued. *No matter what the hour, Susan would have—* He curbed his thoughts sharply. *None of that,* he told himself. *If Jeanette's tired, there's no reason she shouldn't go to bed.*

He went inside, closing the door softly behind him to avoid disturbing her. All was quiet, but a glow of slightly unsteady yellow light from the hall lit his way. He followed it, noting that a faint, sweet odor of violets grew stronger as he approached the master bedroom. He reached its open door and paused.

Candlelight danced on the ceiling. The covers on his side of the bed were turned down invitingly, and a neatly folded pair of his pajamas lay on his pillow. On the other side, propped up by several more pillows, reclined Jeanette, lovely in the pale blue nightgown that she had worn on the first night of their honeymoon. A tiny reading lamp reflected light off the page of scriptures she was reading to softly illuminate her face. Except for her silver-frosted hair, she looked no more than twenty years old.

She looked up and closed the book. "How did it go, honey?"

Andrew crossed the room, sat on the bed, and took her outstretched hand. "Things couldn't be better," he answered.

CHAPTER 3
New Beginnings

Andrew's reasons for taking this day off had included one that he had not been inclined to share with his bishopric: he felt that he needed a little buffer time before leaving the woman he loved to return to the job he hated. Now that his afternoon had been effectively usurped by his new calling, he found it very hard to envision tearing himself away from his bride long enough open the bishop's handbook this morning. He let the call of duty nag at him for a few seconds as he shaved, and then he squelched it. He would take the handbook to work with him this week and read it in spare moments, if necessary. But this time with Jeanette was golden, and he wasn't about to give it up.

Once the two of them had gotten a load of laundry going, they continued their brief honeymoon over a late and leisurely breakfast. Andrew still could not believe the good fortune—providential fortune, in fact—that had brought this sparkling-eyed, pink-cheeked, gorgeous spinster into his life. He wondered how long it would have taken him, a widowed grandfather, to work up the nerve to ask her out if he had not received the mandate to find a bride before being sustained as bishop—and if her house had not burned down and left her virtually destitute on the very day that they met. Given those circumstances, he would have offered her his help and friendship even if they had not been tinged with self-interest. Charity had certainly never been so well rewarded. She was human, of course, and bound to have faults; but he had noticed none, and he was determined not to look for any.

This impression was heightened when, at length, he regretfully admitted to Jeanette that he ought to start telephoning people. "First I'd better get those lunches and dinners lined up for the Barlows."

"No need, darling. I've already done it."

"What?"

"Well, not all of it. When you mentioned it to Rhett, I thought I'd help out. You don't have a Relief Society president yet, and it would take her a while to assemble a board anyway. So I phoned around while you were at your meeting. Gina is taking lunch today, and Sister Jantzen is taking dinner—"

"She's not even in our ward now."

"Casseroles know no borders. Sister Arrowsmith has tomorrow's lunch, Diane Olson has dinner, and Sisters Holmes and Purser are handling the next day. They're all going to write heating instructions down for Rhett. You had the new ward list with you, so I didn't know who else to call, but I figure that you'll have a Relief Society president ready to take it from there—unofficially, of course."

"You're marvelous."

"I just try hard."

"You're succeeding beautifully. I guess the next step is to issue a call to you."

Jeanette looked a little apprehensive. "Re . . . Relief Society president?"

"No," he answered, chuckling. "Family history consultant. Bishop Farr's inspiration was a good one, and we're sticking by it."

Jeanette's eyes shone, and she sighed softly. "I accept. And I'm glad. I had all kinds of ideas to get the work going. And, dear . . ." She hesitated. "Please don't think that I'm trying to influence you, but I've had the strongest feeling that Gina . . . well . . . isn't through with that calling."

"Noted," said Andrew noncommittally, following up with a not-so-noncommittal kiss.

Calling Gina Roylance was, in fact, the first item on Andrew's schedule. During yesterday's meeting, his executive secretary, Todd Mikesell, had begun setting up appointments for him with prospective presidents. Gina's name had deliberately been left off the list. Andrew and Steve had decided last night at the meeting that Andrew, as bishop, ought to be the one to issue the call. Brought up in a tough Chicago neighborhood, Gina could be prickly to deal with, and he wanted to be the one to approach her. Now, with noon imminent, he began walking to the meetinghouse, intending to stop on the way at the Roylance house to see when she could meet with him.

As soon as he turned the corner and entered their street, he could see that chaos was brewing. Two travel-dusty cars heavily laden with baggage stood in the driveway, and the four Roylance children were helping several unfamiliar young people in modish clothing unload them. As Andrew approached, he heard the raised, animated voice of Jake, the eldest Roylance boy, recklessly promising trips to the mountains, the zoo, the planetarium, and every tourist destination in the state. These, then, must be visiting friends or family members.

In the excitement, Andrew made it to the front porch unnoticed. The door was wide open, and the commotion inside was as considerable as that outside. He had to knock loudly to be heard. When Steve came to the door, his customary smile seemed a little careworn.

"I thought you'd be at work, Steve."

"I wish I were. Gina called and begged me to come home when her folks arrived."

"Her parents?"

"No, Gina's still not on speaking terms with them. These are her cousins Vincenzo Modoni and Martina Locatelli and their families, from Chicago."

"The ones who joined the Church and found her on the Internet? I'd heard that they were coming, but I didn't think it was going to be this soon."

"Neither did we. We expected them toward the end of July. The next thing we knew, they'd landed on our doorstep."

"Mmmm . . . This probably isn't a good time to call her as Relief Society president, then."

"Two hours ago might have been better, but later will only be worse. I'll tell her you're here."

He didn't have to. Shouting over her shoulder for everyone to sit down and make themselves at home, Gina elbowed her way to the front door, looking more harassed than ever. She was carrying a covered kettle with both hands, and dangling from her wrist was a plastic bag containing what appeared to be wrapped sandwiches. "Bishop, did you bring your car?" she asked without preamble.

"Sorry, but I'm on foot," Andrew began.

"Vinnie? Pete? I lied," she yelled over her shoulder again. "One of you needs to move a car for me."

"My car's out at the curb," Steve murmured.

"Vinnie? Pete? I lied again," she bellowed. "Sit down. Sarah, come with us." She cut off her older daughter's attempt to protest before it could begin. "You'll need to know where to get the kettle back from." To Steve she muttered hurriedly, "Hold the fort while I'm gone. If Pete lights up a cigarette, throw him out. Bishop, you come with us. Steve, he'll need your car keys."

Andrew waited until they were in the car to ask, "Where am I taking you?"

"Barlows', of course," she snapped. "And hurry. That lot can trash a house in three minutes flat."

Andrew started the ignition, wondering how to broach the subject of an interview. His indecision lasted barely a moment.

"Sarah, plug your ears for a minute," Gina ordered. "Never mind why." Once Sarah's fingers were obediently stuck into her ears, Gina lowered her voice an almost imperceptible notch and continued. "Steve hinted that you'd want to meet with me. Let's save time. Yes, I accept the call."

"Do you know what it is?" Andrew asked, wondering what the bishop's handbook had to say about such an unconventional setting and procedure for an interview.

"Relief Society president. And don't go thinking that Steve talked me into it. I've known it from the moment you were called as bishop."

"How?"

"Because I'm not having a good time yet," she answered cryptically.

Andrew had already turned the second of the two corners that took them to the far side of the block. Now he pulled in front of the shabby little rental home occupied by the Barlows. Sarah hadn't even gotten her fingers out of her ears before Gina was out and halfway up the sidewalk. Andrew had to run to reach the doorbell before she shoved the front door open with one foot and marched in.

"Soup's hot and ready," she announced to a startled Rhett. "Paper plates and bowls are in the bag with the sandwiches. Sorry we can't stay to help feed the babies, but we had company from out of town arrive unexpectedly. I'll send Sarah"—she gestured at Sarah, who had burst through the door just in time to be introduced—"to pick up the kettle this evening. Don't bother washing it—we'll do that. My phone number's on a piece of paper in the bag. Post it on your fridge, and call me if you need anything. If I don't hear from you in three days, I'll call you. Tell Tif we miss her."

She was out the door again before Andrew could say more than, "This is Sister Gina Roylance." He stayed long enough to add, "And she means what she says. If you don't call her, she will call you." With a hasty good-bye, he ran back to the car, where Gina was already in the passenger's seat.

"You can leave your ears unplugged," she told Sarah, who was still clambering into the backseat, "but whatever you hear is none of anyone's business but mine, okay?" Sarah, to whom this was apparently nothing new, immediately began singing a jazzed-up version of "When We're Helping, We're Happy" as a sound barrier. Gina addressed Andrew. "What else has been arranged for them?"

He might as well follow Sarah's example and go with the flow. "Two more days of lunch and dinner," he reported as he started the car. "We've committed to at least four more days beyond that."

"What about child care?"

"The grandmothers are handling it."

"Good. Tif was breast-feeding. Who's collecting her milk for the baby?"

Andrew could feel himself blush. "Uh . . ."

"Never mind. I'll call the hospital and work things out. And I'll call Jeanette and get details on the meal assignments. I assume she arranged all that."

It wasn't a question, but Andrew answered yes.

"Where will you be this afternoon?"

"At the bish—at my office at church."

"I'll phone you the names of some people to interview as soon as I get everyone settled. We'll have the rest chosen by tomorrow evening. I'll give those names to Steve. Okay, Sarah, you're free," she stated as Andrew parked Steve's car in front of the Roylance home. Gratefully, Sarah broke off her song and rocketed out the back door. As Gina exited, she glanced over her shoulder and remarked, "Jeanette was my first choice as a counselor, you know. But the Lord said no."

* * *

Andrew had said that he would be home no later than six o'clock. With plenty of free time on her hands, Jeanette took an inventory of the kitchen cupboards and refrigerator and made a sizable grocery list. Next, she went to the basement and checked out the food storage situation. As she had suspected, it was beautifully organized, labeled, and dated. Shelves of cans, glinting Mason jars of fruit, buckets of staple foods, and large containers of water stood in neat rows, though it looked as if rotation and restocking had been haphazard for the past three years. *Ever since Susan died,* she mused as she began lists of what needed to be used right away and what needed to be replenished.

She had just finished and was on her way up when she saw a distinctive set of binders in a small bookcase near the bottom of the stairs. They were thick with dust—three to four years' worth, she judged. *Interesting,* she thought. *Especially in view of Andrew's first words to me. I wonder if he really meant them.* Impulsively, she grabbed the binders, blew off the dust, and took them upstairs to examine. As she did so, ideas began to form in her head. They felt right, but not necessarily comfortable. They might lay a few ghosts to rest, or they might come back to haunt her for a lifetime. As she read and pondered, her rising level of anxiety led her to understand that she was onto something very important to her personally. She also knew that if she let herself consider the consequences for too long, she would lose her nerve. *Trying to scare me out of it, Mr. Satan? Then it's definitely on,* she concluded, closing the binders and setting them on a shelf in a closet. *I'll do it tonight.*

After comparing her lists, she boldly returned downstairs and selected a single Mason jar, its golden contents slightly darkened by age. Then she got into the car to head for the grocery store. On her way, though, she stopped in at West Park Regional to visit Tiffany Barlow.

Tiffany was awake and all enthusiasm. "Look at this!" she exclaimed, wiggling all ten toes frantically. "And this!" She flexed her feet. "And this!" She bent one knee. "The other would bend too if it weren't for the splint. Oh, I was *so* scared when I woke up from surgery! It felt like someone was crushing my legs in chicken wire, and I yelled at them to stop. But the doctor told me to enjoy the pain, because it meant I could feel again, and that meant I'd be able to walk again. You know what? I'll *never* complain about pain again as long as I live!

"And the nicest lady just called me to tell me all about how the Relief Society ladies are helping Rhett out. She's going to have a nurse store my milk for the baby as soon as the medications are out of my system. And Mom just called me to say that the kids are doing fine, and she's done two loads of laundry for me . . ."

Tiffany effervesced for a good half hour and would have continued longer had a nurse not intervened and ushered Jeanette out. "If we can get her to rest, she'll be able to go home by the end of the week," the woman confided to Jeanette. "Things will be pretty dull around here after that."

Shopping, restocking, and finishing the laundry took the rest of the afternoon. By the time Andrew arrived home at five thirty, dinner was well underway. He had never had shish kebabs on wild rice before, and he was full of praise. The interviewing had gone well, and he was clearly excited about some of the leadership in the new ward. Even handling the welfare emergencies and spiritual crises had gone unexpectedly smoothly. "If I thought that being a bishop would be this pleasant all the time," he concluded, "I'd be blissfully happy. Since I know it won't be, I'm going to enjoy times like this to the fullest."

Jeanette smiled adoringly at him, pleased that her carefully prepared meal had added to his enjoyment. But the moment of truth was fast arriving. "Since you've been so busy, I took the liberty of preparing the lesson for home evening," she began tentatively. "We haven't really had time to discuss topics, so I hope you don't mind my taking the lead."

"Not at all," he said expansively.

"We'll need to clear the table," she said as she rose.

She managed to prolong the moment by filling the dishwasher, starting it, and putting a thoughtfully prepared peach cobbler into the oven to bake. By the time she had retrieved her laptop computer and a hymnal for the opening song, she was having a hard time keeping her hands from shaking visibly. She wondered if it was too late to change lesson topics. But then the book fell open in her hands to the hymn "Turn Your Hearts." She drew a long breath and said, as casually as she could, "Let's sing this one."

The hymn and prayer were a blur. Filling in their electronic calendars was something of a letdown, since it showed that she would see nearly nothing of Andrew until Friday evening. Then it was her turn. "Do you remember," she began in a tone that tried to be lighthearted, "what we discussed in our very first conversation?"

"Family history," Andrew replied promptly, to her great surprise.

"Well . . . ah . . . I just wondered," Jeanette began. She paused, then the words tumbled out in a heedless rush. "Did you really want to learn about it? Or was it just a convenient pickup line?" Aghast, she clapped a hand to her mouth.

"Yes and yes," Andrew responded, his eyes twinkling. "I've wanted and needed to learn about it for a long time. But if you had been promoting skydiving as a technique for better appreciating the plan of salvation, I'd have been first in line to sign up. I know we never got around to your actually teaching me anything, but things did get pretty busy after that, between Gina's curfew and the war games and overtime at the base . . ."

"And Chief Ridley with his mysterious corpses," recalled Jeanette with a squeaky sort of giggle.

Andrew reached over and took her hand. "You've been nervous all evening, sweetheart. What's up?"

"Just . . . silly insecurities, I guess," she admitted, blinking back tears. "I-I found your genealogy binders downstairs today—

yours and Susan's. There's . . . a lot of memories you two shared, and . . ." Her voice trailed off.

"And you figure you can't compete?" Andrew sighed. "Oh, Jeanette, I should have realized it would be hard for you. I suppose I got too wrapped up in my own happiness. Listen here, you innocent young thing, haven't you ever read *Persuasion*?"

"Well . . . of course," Jeanette began, puzzled. "But what . . ."

"Well, I haven't, but I watched the movie once with Susan. Do you remember the scene where that thickheaded Wentworth is listening in while Anne and Captain What's-his-name—Harvard, or something like that—are talking about the differences between men and women in love?"

"Captain Harville? Yes . . ."

"So the words that Jane Austen put into their mouths hit the nail square on the head. When a spouse dies, women seem to live for years on memories. Most men can't do that. We're . . . too earthy, I guess. Memories tantalize us, frustrate us. That's why I stopped going places and doing things that Susan and I used to do. It was too hard to do alone. Keeping the binders up to date was Susan's hobby—she didn't research things the way you do, but she'd add new information whenever she could get it. I haven't opened a family history binder since Susan died—not even to add Fiona's marriage," he added, struck suddenly by his own lack of initiative. "Sheri's been after me for months about it, but I just couldn't bring myself to face the memories. It would have been like losing her again."

Jeanette could think of nothing to say.

"But now you're here. I can delve into those books and face those memories, and when I close them, you'll still be here, ready to love me." He paused, looking expectantly into her face.

She didn't quite understand, but his words were comforting. She smiled tremulously.

"So, let's hit those binders. Show me where I come from," Andrew said energetically.

Soon both binders were open on the table, and Andrew was identifying the generation in each of his lines that had first embraced the gospel. "There. Peder Skriver, born in Denmark and died in Nephi, Utah. And this one—wow, born in Nauvoo! I didn't know about that."

"We'll get to know them all much better as we enter the information into a computer database," Jeanette remarked.

"Gone paperless, have we?"

"Not completely. But searching and comparing data on computers is a lot easier than on paper. And if we find any ancestors who need temple work done, their information has to be submitted electronically."

Andrew measured the thickness of his binder between his thumb and index finger. "That's going to be a year's worth of data entry, at the rate I type," he lamented. "Isn't there a faster way?"

"No, dear. And that's part of the Lord's plan. We need to dwell on them long enough to know them, to wonder about their lives. Otherwise they're just names on paper, and our hearts can't be turned toward them. But if you promise to study them carefully," she added, smiling mischievously, "maybe you can offer me some well-chosen incentives to type them in for you."

"Do you mean that I should *bribe* you?" Andrew demanded in mock indignation.

They examined Susan's binder as well, but Andrew soon laid it aside. "I'm going to loan this one to Sheri. She's been dying to enter Eric's side of their family into her database. This will give her something to do. And just maybe she'll forgive me for putting her off for so long."

Jeanette wasn't taken in by the reasoning, but she appreciated the thought.

Andrew was fumblingly beginning to enter his and his children's data into a new file on Jeanette's computer when the stove timer sounded. "Smells great," he commented as Jeanette pulled the cobbler from the oven. But when he tasted his portion, served with vanilla ice cream melting into the crumbly topping, he stopped short and looked searchingly at Jeanette. She looked down in confusion.

"A test?" he queried.

Reluctantly, she nodded.

He smacked his lips thoughtfully. "The best peach cobbler filling I've ever tasted," he stated judiciously, "and the best topping. Made by the two finest cooks in the world—and the two most beautiful. Do I pass?"

She nodded again, smiling.

He rose and enfolded her in his arms. "Does that mean I get to kiss one of the cooks?"

Their lips had barely met when the front door burst open. In stalked Mark, his eyes downcast. They broke apart, but he didn't appear to notice them.

"Mark?" Andrew asked.

No response.

"I thought you were attending home evening with Alyssa's family tonight."

"Huh," Mark grunted.

"Did it fall through?"

A long pause. Then a strange, muffled, bitter voice replied. "Not the evening. Just . . . the wedding." He raised reddened eyes to meet his father's shocked look. "The wedding's off," he repeated more loudly. "Her parents have withdrawn their consent." Then his gaze fell on the table, with its load of genealogy binders. He stiffened and pointed at the binders accusingly. "And *that's* why."

CHAPTER 4
Love Lost

The story came out in bits and pieces as Jeanette and Andrew wheedled it from him. The home evening at the Jarvis residence had begun amicably enough. The object of the lesson had been to introduce Mark to his fiancée's family heritage. The trouble had begun with a seemingly innocuous comment that Mark himself had made.

"All I said was that I had a Thomas and Mary Barnes in my ancestry too," he mourned, "and that they had a son named John. Then Sister Jarvis got upset and began asking me a bunch of strange questions. Brother Jarvis got on the Internet and began doing all kinds of weird searches. The next thing I knew, they were telling me that Alyssa and I are first cousins, so we can't get married."

"*First cousins?*" Andrew almost shouted. "That isn't possible! How could you be first cousins and not know it?"

"Alyssa's mom is adopted," Mark explained dully. "She's just discovered her biological lineage."

"And that's where the problem is," guessed Jeanette.

"Uh-huh."

"But first cousins get married all the time in novels," protested Andrew.

"In English novels," amended Jeanette. "In America, most states have a law against first-cousin marriages. In Utah—"

"In Utah," Mark broke in, his voice taking on a sarcastically high intonation and singsong inflection, "'first cousins who are sixty-five years of age or older can marry without consent. First cousins who are fifty-five years of age or older will need to provide documentation to the district court that they are incapable of reproduction.' Brother Jarvis found the law on the Internet." He slumped in his chair. "Like I could ask Alyssa to wait thirty-five years and never have any children. Right."

"How is Alyssa taking this?" Andrew asked.

"About like I am. She's devastated. Even as much as we love each other, she'll never marry anyone without her parents' blessing. And I can't ask her to choose between us."

Jeanette's heart hurt desperately for him. "Well," she began hesitantly, "if Brother Jarvis found Utah's law on the Internet, he also found that there are states that do allow first-cousin marriages under age fifty-five. And lots of them have temples. Genetic problems aren't as big an issue as they used to be when people didn't move from place to place as much. They don't usually crop up unless it's a very self-contained community with a high proportion of cousin intermarriages."

Mark shook his head miserably. "There's more to it than that. They told me some big story about somebody's uncle who married a first cousin and it didn't work out. All the relatives took sides, and it split the family up so badly that nobody will talk to anybody else."

"A feud?" asked Andrew.

"Yes, and they won't even consider getting their family involved in the same thing. But that wouldn't happen to *us*!" he burst out desperately, bouncing to the edge of his chair. "Alyssa and I are meant for each other. I tell you, when I first saw her, it was like I recognized her, like I'd known her forever. And I didn't even see her face! She was at the front of the classroom, and I was at the back. But every move she made—it was familiar, like a memory. I knew what her voice would sound like, how she would walk—if ever any two people were meant to be together, we were. And now this." He slumped back into the depths of his chair, fighting back the tears.

Jeanette let her own tears flow. Andrew rose, walked over to his son, and pulled him out of the chair into a long, comforting embrace. "You're staying the night," he said finally, "and as many nights as you need to. I'll find you some pajamas and a toothbrush."

While Andrew began rummaging through drawers, Jeanette made Mark a cup of hot chocolate.

"I'm not thirsty," he said, waving it away.

"This isn't for thirst. It's liquid comfort—medicine. Drink it," she urged.

He drank, but she knew it was only because he was too exhausted by grief to put up a struggle. She sat in silence, her forehead creased thoughtfully, as he slowly drained the cup. Putting it down on a side table, he leaned forward, elbows on his knees, and stared unseeingly at the carpet. "Nan," he said at last, using the pet name that he and his siblings called her, "how could God let us meet and fall in love and then rip us apart like this? How could He?"

Jeanette looked up and spoke the thoughts that had been filling her head for the past ten minutes. "I don't believe that He did, Mark. The more I think this over, the more I feel as if someone is jumping to conclusions too quickly. There are an awful lot of Thomas and Mary Barneses in the world, and I'll bet that a good number of them named a son John. Would you be willing to tell me a few details, or would you rather wait until morning?"

He shook his head involuntarily at the word *wait,* so she pressed forward. "Which side of your ancestry are your Thomas and Mary Barnes on?"

"Mom's, I think," he muttered.

Jeanette rose and picked up Susan's binder. The offending couple were on Susan's maternal line, in the Utah pioneer generation.

"These people came from somewhere in England, exact town unknown. How about those in Sister Jarvis's line?"

"Same."

"Did their Thomas and Mary have any children besides John?"

"No." He looked up hopefully.

"Neither did these," she admitted reluctantly, and he lowered his head again. "Where in Utah did they live?"

"Centerville."

"So did these." She sighed and studied the book carefully. "It says here that John married Annie Rogers and moved to Farmington. Their son, Joseph Lehi, married Rose Davis. Their daughter, Bertha Lillian, married Lyle Rodney Newman in Salt Lake City in 1926. Does any of that sound like what you saw in the Jarvises' records?"

Mark groaned deeply. "I remember the names Rogers, Lehi, and Lyle, and something about Farmington. I can't remember the rest, but I know that Mom's mother was a Newman."

"Did Sister Jarvis have an undisputed line from herself back to this couple?"

"What do you mean by *undisputed*?"

"Does she have documentation proving every generation of it? Birth certificates, ward records, census records, things like that?"

Mark pondered, then he looked up quickly. "Most of it came from some other lady's research. I don't think she had anything older than her own certificate of adoption."

Andrew had returned, pajamas in hand, in time to hear most of this exchange. Now he spoke eagerly. "So most of what she's got is hearsay?"

"It sounds like it," Jeanette agreed. "It could be entirely accurate, or it could be somebody's guess that was never thoroughly researched and proven."

"So there's a chance—" Andrew began.

"—that it's wrong?" Mark finished, his eyes gleaming excitedly.

"It's worth pursuing," Jeanette concluded. "I'll call the Jarvises in the morning and see if they'll let me take a look at their records."

Mark bounced out of his chair. "Del and Irene. Their number is 768-2493."

"There is another way to know conclusively, but it would take time and cost some money."

"Conclusive results would be worth it," Mark said fervently, and Andrew nodded. "What do we do?"

"A mitochondrial DNA test. But getting the results back could take weeks or even months, and it's likely to cost between a hundred and three hundred dollars."

Mark stopped short, his face pained. Jeanette knew that three hundred dollars constituted the entire budget for the honeymoon he had planned. Gently, she added, "We'd have to talk Irene Jarvis into participating, too. And since Susan can't participate, Fiona would need to take her place."

"What does it involve?" Andrew asked. "Fio's pregnant, remember."

"Nothing very big—either a blood test or a swab of epithelial tissue from the inside of a cheek. Lab technicians would compare the results they get from Irene and Fiona. If Irene and Susan were really born to the same mother, Irene's mtDNA and Fiona's should be identical."

"What's the chance of a flawed test?"

"If the company doing the analysis is reliable, it's virtually nonexistent. But it's got to be done by skilled and well-trained people. There are few enough companies in the business that they can charge pretty well whatever they like, and they've always got a backlog of requests."

Andrew glanced at his son. "If it will prove this conclusively, let's do it. I'll foot the bill."

Jeanette nodded. "And I'll see if I can talk Irene into it."

Mark bounded to the phone. "I'll call Fio. I know she'll help."

Fiona was deeply sympathetic and very eager to help. She was familiar with the process and offered to provide a kit from the hospital that Jeanette could pick up the following morning. But her estimate of the time frame was even less optimistic than Jeanette's.

"A *year*!" Mark gulped as he hung up the phone. "I could go stark raving mad in that amount of time—even if some other guy hasn't snapped her up before then." He froze and then gasped aloud. "Oh no! She was dating Bill Ross until he left for a tour with the military. He's due home in a month! If he gets back into the picture, I'll be history."

"Who's Bill Ross?" asked Jeanette, glancing from Andrew's troubled face to Mark's pained one.

Andrew answered heavily, "He was the former wrestling team captain at the kids' high school. He dated Fiona a few times. A bit brain-deficient, in my opinion, but physically a very handsome young man."

"He could double for that drop-dead-gorgeous opera guy, George Dyer," Mark concurred with a moan.

Jeanette knew exactly who that was. The comparison was daunting, but she couldn't bear to see the cloud of despondency settling over Mark again. "We may be able to settle it faster the old-fashioned way, using research." She looked appealingly at Andrew.

"Let's do both," proposed Andrew. "We'll send the samples in for testing, but we'll go ahead with the research while we're waiting. The sooner we come up with something conclusive, the better."

* * *

Jeanette had barely made it out of bed the next morning before the phone rang. "Jeanette? We need your help," Gina said by way of greeting. "Vinnie's records don't match Marti's, and neither of them match mine."

A major purpose of this visit from Gina's recently baptized relatives was to compare family history information. Apparently, Gina had lost no time. Jeanette wondered that she hadn't gotten a call last night at midnight or so.

"I can be there in . . . about an hour," Jeanette responded, checking her alarm clock and calculating quickly.

Gina sighed exasperatedly into the phone. "We'll be waiting."

Once she had dressed and breakfasted, Jeanette placed a call to the Jarvis residence. Irene Jarvis was a pleasant and friendly woman, but she seemed a little distressed on hearing Jeanette's errand. "Of course, you're welcome to come over and see the records. But I'm afraid that we can't negotiate on this matter. We dearly love Mark, and this has been very disappointing to all of us, but blood is blood."

Except when it isn't, thought Jeanette obstinately. Aloud she said, "We genealogists just can't resist records. Thank you for letting me come." Not knowing how long it would take to provide the help Gina wanted, Jeanette set the appointment for two in the afternoon. She decided to wait until she was face-to-face with Irene to broach the suggestion of a DNA test.

Half an hour later, at the Roylances' front door, Jeanette raised a hand to ring the bell and paused, listening apprehensively to loud, rapid-paced voices emanating from within. She could not quite make out the words, but it sounded like nothing so much as a fight in progress. Andrew had mentioned a sense of tension in the air when he had visited the Roylances the other day. She hoped that the newly rekindled relationship between Gina and her cousins wasn't about to explode into open warfare. Gulping as the voices rose and overlapped, she rang the bell and prepared to retreat in haste if necessary.

Gina herself came to the door. "Right on time. Come in."

"I'm not . . . interrupting anything, am I?"

"No, we're just talking."

Jeanette entered, her eyes round, to see every seat in the living room filled with dark-haired, olive-skinned adults, all jabbering away in a mixture of English and Italian. There seemed to be at least as many different conversations going on as there were people, and no one seemed to know or care whether he or she was actually being listened to.

"Haven't had a good family discussion like this in ages," Gina confided. "The kids were in here as well, but they were too noisy. We sent them to take a tour of the neighborhood."

"Everyone seems to have hit it off well," Jeanette observed, relieved.

"Just like old times—including Pete over there, feeling his pockets for cigarettes." Gina smirked ungenerously. "He's agreed to keep them in the car while they're visiting. That way, he'll remember to go outside to smoke."

During the two hours that followed, Jeanette noticed that Pete did indeed have a habit of pawing at his shirt's front pocket, which hung loosely, as if it were accustomed to being filled to capacity. Three times during Jeanette's visit, he excused himself and headed outside. Each time, he returned after about ten minutes, smelling like a brush fire in the fields of old Virginia. Each time, Gina wrinkled her nose and pursed her lips but said nothing.

The cousins' information conflicted slightly, coming as it did from their memories.

"I know for sure that Great-Grandpapa Luciano had ten kids, counting the two that died," Vinnie asserted.

"Who says? Aunt Giustina told me he had twelve," Marti quickly countered.

"Well, Uncle Berto said ten, and who'd know Luciano better than his nephew?" Vinnie argued.

"His own granddaughter might," Marti concluded, "and that's Aunt Giustina!"

"You're all wet, both of you," cut in Gina. "He had seven that lived and four that died as infants. Mom told me that when I was three years old."

"What would she know? She was only his step-cousin," objected Vinnie.

"Twice removed," Marti chimed in.

Obviously, all this information dated from long before any of them had begun taking an interest in the details. After studying the records, Jeanette suggested various possible sources to check to resolve these differences. Like a general planning a campaign, Gina handed out assignments to everyone present, to be filled on an upcoming visit to the Family History Library in Salt Lake City. Her cousins and their spouses seemed to take this as a matter of course. Impressed into service, Jeanette accepted her share along with everyone else. *Gina's a natural leader,* she thought. *That's what makes her such a good Relief Society president.* She hoped that Andrew would seriously consider the impression she had shared with him the day before.

Eventually, the discussion turned to what activities might entertain the families during their stay. "We'll need to stay close to home this week," Gina explained. "The ward's just been reorganized. Jeanette's husband is the new bishop, and Steve is one of his counselors. They need to get things set up for Sunday."

Both Marti and Pete looked at Jeanette with new interest. "Your husband's the bishop?" they chorused, then looked suspiciously at each other.

"Yes," Jeanette acknowledged.

"That's a big job for a man," Marti remarked. The family resemblance to Gina was unmistakable—she had the same thin face and strong features, along with an echo of Gina's authoritative manner. "You probably won't see much of him this week, will you?"

"Very little, I'm afraid. He'll be interviewing people at his office at the church till ten o'clock every night this week."

"Mmm," said Pete thoughtfully. He seemed like a man who wasn't used to much serious thinking—the kind who preferred to enjoy life. Jeanette could picture him hanging out with "the boys" on a regular basis. It was interesting that he had chosen Marti as a wife; the two of them appeared to be as opposite as it was possible for two personalities to be. *Maybe they balance each other out,* Jeanette thought.

"Speaking of the time, I assume you've set a curfew, Gina. What is it? We need to let the kids know," remarked Vinnie, leaning casually back in his armchair. Jeanette smiled inwardly, curious to see what Gina's big-city cousins would make of her idea of nightlife.

"Nine o'clock, but we can stretch it to nine thirty since school's out."

If Gina had dropped a bomb, she could not have caused more of a sensation. Every one of her cousins went from relaxed to bolt-upright in a heartbeat.

"*Nine thirty!* Are you crazy?" exclaimed Vinnie.

"Vinnie, that's rude," reproved his wife. She had been introduced as Caterina but had immediately abbreviated the name to Cat. "But, Gina, dear," she continued anxiously, "Isn't it . . . uh . . . unsafe?"

Jeanette eyes widened again. She had been expecting the word *unreasonable.*

"Yeah," Pete agreed. "Don't the streets get dangerous at about seven?"

"Not here," Gina responded smugly.

Marti leaned forward. "You've got to be kidding. No drunk drivers? No street gangs? No gunfire?"

"Oh, that stuff goes on in some places, yeah. But you saw the overpasses. How much graffiti was there? And how many bars and lounges did you count on the way here? I can tell you this much: I haven't heard a gunshot within city limits since I moved here seventeen years ago."

The Honeymoon's Over

Her guests looked at each other with undisguised amazement. "Mmm," mused Pete once again.

"Well, could we keep curfew at nine o'clock, just for the sake of my nerves?" asked Cat.

"And mine?" Marti chimed in.

"If you like," Gina conceded.

* * *

Andrew hurried home after work, not just to be on time for the full evening of interviews scheduled for him after dinner, but also to hear what Jeanette had learned about Irene Jarvis's family history. Mark arrived from work a split second after he did, and they entered the door together. "Hi, sweetheart," Andrew began, greeting Jeanette with a kiss.

Mark showed a good deal less decorum and more impatience. "What's the news, Nan?"

Jeanette's smile of welcome showed a touch of stress. "Not all bad, but not conclusive either. Irene and I had a talk, and she printed out copies of her biological line for me. It's exactly like Susan's, line for line—" She paused as Mark uttered a stricken cry, then hurried on. "But there's no documentation noted."

"What does that mean?" asked Andrew, glancing at Mark.

"It means that there are no certificates or records backing up any of the claims. Just as you said, she hasn't got anything but her certificate of adoption."

"Then how does Irene figure that it's really her line?" Andrew demanded.

"Well, when she began the search . . . uh . . . what if we have dinner first?" Jeanette suggested, her voice trembling a little.

Andrew moved toward the table, but Mark would not be dissuaded. "If you're not ready to tell me, then it's bad, isn't it?" he guessed despondently.

"Not entirely. But first, please promise me that you'll eat," Jeanette begged.

Mark promised.

When a blessing had been offered and the dinner served, Jeanette spoke again, softly. "Remember, Mark, this is only the beginning. I intend to search the entire line, and I won't accept any link that hasn't got plenty of authentic information to back it up. But Irene began her search by accessing her adoption file. It indicates that she was born in Cedar City, Utah, to a young woman who was staying in a town nearby called Parowan, at the home of her brother and his wife. Supposedly, her husband was away serving in the Korean War, but for reasons that weren't specified in the file, she relinquished all parental rights. The brother notified a relative of his wife's who knew a couple that had been childless for a long time and wanted a daughter. This couple drove down to Parowan to get the baby."

"That still doesn't—" Mark protested.

"The name of the young woman's brother was Cleve Kirk Newman, and his wife's name was Charlotte."

Andrew choked on a sip of milk and coughed until tears streamed from his eyes. There couldn't be that many Cleve Kirk Newmans in the entire world, let alone in Parowan.

"Newman?" Mark asked in obvious dread.

Jeanette hesitated, glanced at Andrew, and continued gravely. "I called your mom's cousin Russ Newman this afternoon. He and your mom had an uncle Cleve Kirk Newman who married Charlotte Snow and lived out his life in Parowan. Russ also told me something that he said your mom never knew. Her mother, Linda, was engaged to a young man in 1950, but they broke it off. Soon afterward, she went to stay with her brother Cleve and his new wife in Parowan. She told her family that she wanted to get away from the memories. She was gone for nearly a year."

Andrew stopped eating, suddenly sick to his stomach. "Are you saying that she . . ." He couldn't finish.

The Honeymoon's Over

Jeanette lowered her head. "It's circumstantial, but the facts and the dates all match. If it's true, Irene Jarvis and Susan are half-sisters."

Mark laid down his silverware and began to push his plate away. Remembering his promise, he grimaced and began shoveling food into his mouth. Andrew could tell that he was swallowing it without tasting it. He himself had lost his appetite completely. The idea that Susan's elegant, ladylike, spiritually minded mother had borne a child out of wedlock was incomprehensible to him. "Did Irene consent to the DNA test?" he asked anxiously.

"Not at first, but I think it was because she didn't understand it. Once I explained that it just meant swabbing the inside of her cheek, she was fine with it. But she didn't think it would make any difference in the end. I took the swab, and Fiona will send it with hers tomorrow to whichever company can offer the best turnaround." Jeanette turned again to Mark. "But I haven't given up," she told him. "I intend to track down every possible record to find out what really happened. Something still doesn't seem right. For one thing, Irene doesn't look anything like Susan or Russ. But it could take a while. The only other information I've been able to get this afternoon is that everyone who could tell me anything firsthand about this matter is dead—Susan's mother, Susan's uncle, and his wife."

Mark whimpered like a lost soul and turned away from the table. Jeanette laid a gentle hand on his arm. "If it helps you feel any better," she added consolingly, "Irene was in tears about you for most of my visit. She and Del feel terrible about this, and they both want you to know that they didn't withdraw their consent because of any objection they have to you. In fact, she says that they've never met a finer young man, and she's honored to have you as a nephew."

Mark opened his mouth, seemed to reconsider, and closed it somberly.

"I saw Alyssa for a moment, too. She was on her way to Dutch's Diner, where she used to work. They were happy to hire her back, she said, but she didn't seem very happy herself—about that or anything else."

A thunderous, familiar knock put an end to the discussion.

"Chief Ridley, as I live and breathe," muttered Andrew darkly as he rose from the table.

"Hi, folks," the chief called, stepping in as soon as Andrew opened the door. "Dinner smells great, but I can't stay. Gotta help with Tif's kids this evening. Just stopped by to see if you can give me a hand again. Remember the corpse in that grave the dog was guarding?"

Andrew remembered all too well. So did Jeanette, judging from the look on her face. She was the one who had first suspected that the canine intruder in a local backyard was standing watch over more than just a lumpy, weedy patch of failed garden. A police excavation on the spot had proved her instincts gruesomely correct. Even Mark looked up, momentarily diverted from his own problems.

"We've had two developments—kind of baffling. Put a whole new light on the case. First one is that the autopsy results came back today."

This time it was Jeanette who laid down her fork and pushed her plate away, her face turning visibly pale.

"Chief, can this wait?" Andrew demanded.

"Won't be but a second more. He died of a coronary. Body got kind of banged up, but all postmortem, see, so death was natural. But the second thing is we finally tracked his family. They're in Vegas, and they had no clue he was dead. Or that's how it appears, anyway. Only the kids speak enough English to be understood, but the mom and grandma are crying and howling like they've lost the prop and stay of their whole existence. Big ugly brute like that . . . well, tastes differ, I guess. But the thing is we've got a whole new crime on our hands."

Andrew felt unaccountably stupid. "But if he died naturally, how is it a crime?"

"'Cause he was buried secretly in an unapproved grave, of course! Desecration of a corpse—not to mention breaking the sanitation bylaws into smithereens. If it was his family that'd buried him, we could put it down to ignorance of the law, see, them being immigrants and all. But they didn't even know he was dead; they took a bus to Vegas expecting to meet him there. I haven't questioned 'em yet, of course, but the detective I sent is a sharp one, and she's convinced they aren't playacting. So that grave he was in is a crime scene after all but not the way we thought."

"That poor family!" Jeanette breathed.

"Yeah," Chief Ridley agreed. "I'm having the detective drive them back up here for more questioning and formal ID of the body. Problem is that they can't speak English. They're from . . . Slo-something. Some place in eastern Europe."

"Slovakia?" Andrew hazarded.

"Naw, another Slo-something."

"Slovenia," Jeanette supplied.

"That's it. You Mormons are always sending your kids to lots of far-out places, so I wondered if you know anyone who speaks Slovenlyan, or whatever it is. I'd ask Rick Farr, but he's back East."

From his service on the stake high council, Andrew was acquainted with pretty well every man and woman in the immediate area who had served a mission over the past several years. None of them had gone to Slovenia. "I'm sorry, but I don't know of anyone. How about you, Jeanette?"

She shook her head.

Mark pressed one fist against his apparently aching head. "I do." He sighed morosely. "Del and Irene Jarvis."

CHAPTER 5
Secrets

DURING A RARE LULL IN the constant stream of interviews that Tuesday evening, Andrew rested his head in his hands. So many problems! He hadn't realized that the smooth surface of a stake could hide all these undercurrents of trouble. Already he'd dealt with three more emergency food orders and counseled two families in the throes of debt foreclosures. There hadn't been any divorce requests so far, but one active high priest had come in demanding that the new bishop rescind the temple recommend of an estranged relative—another active high priest—whose home had been included in the new ward by the boundary change. It had taken all of Andrew's patience and tact to explain the basics of Christian charity to this man who was supposed to be charged with teaching it. And it had taken all his forbearance to keep from confiscating the mulish man's own temple recommend. He wondered idly what had caused the breach between them. A soured marriage of first cousins, perhaps?

His thoughts reverted to Mark's dilemma. With the martyred air of one sprinkling salt on his own wounds, his son, after returning from work that afternoon, had courageously telephoned the Jarvises himself, accepted their jumbled apologies with a show of grace, and enlisted their aid for Chief Ridley. Then he had retired to his room, to which Jeanette, after hastily kissing her departing husband farewell, had quickly followed him. Gratitude welled up in Andrew as he thought of her. What an angel! She would mother Mark, cheer him, tap the springs of hope in his broken heart.

A solid rap on the door announced the next arrival. Mercifully, this interviewee and the two following him had no problems worse than a dead car battery among them—or, at least, none that they shared with him. They accepted new callings eagerly and left with dispatch, allowing him another period of rest. It lasted about forty-five seconds before elevated, emphatic voices in the next office reached his ears. They lasted for about a minute. Then, following a tap on the connecting door, Sam Taylor, his new ward clerk, sullenly ushered in one of Gina's cousins.

"Oh, stop sniveling!" she told Sam. "He's a bishop. It's his job. It's not like I can fly back to Chicago to talk to mine."

The expression on Sam's face as he closed the door told Andrew that he bet this woman could fly and that he was willing to supply the broom. Andrew stood to shake her hand.

"Sister Modoni, is it? Or Sister Locatelli?"

"Locatelli," she answered as if the name was slightly distasteful. "Call me Marti."

Using the first name of a strange woman did not accord well with the unspoken etiquette of a bishop's office, but she had given the instruction as an order. Andrew resolved to compromise by not using her name unless it became necessary. He supposed that the Locatellis had left some important item at home and needed help replenishing it here.

Marti sat down and got directly to the point. "It's about Pete."

"Peat," Andrew echoed blankly. He wasn't sure that the bishop's storehouse commodities even included such an item, and he definitely didn't know why a vacationer from Chicago would need it.

"My husband," she added, as if realizing belatedly by Andrew's baffled look that not everyone on earth knew Pete by name. "Pietro Locatelli."

"Oh, yes. Gina mentioned him when I was over yesterday," Andrew offered, trying to make up for lost ground.

"Nothing good, I presume."

"Uh . . ."

"That's why I'm here. I'd like the name of a lawyer who can keep a secret."

Apprehensively, Andrew spoke the obvious. "Steve Roylance."

"Not Steve, for the love of Mike! It was hard enough sneaking in here without him noticing me. Do you think I want to start a riot?"

"I'm still not sure what you want," Andrew replied honestly, his uneasiness growing.

"I want someone who will help me turn Pete around. I'm going to file for divorce."

Here it was. Andrew sat back, fishing for inspiration.

But Marti hadn't finished. "I want a lawyer who can threaten well and get him to listen seriously. But whoever it is has to understand that we're not going to follow through, no matter what."

"You're going to threaten to divorce Pete but not actually do it?"

"That's right." She too sat back, waiting.

There must be a reason, but darned if I see it, thought Andrew. Then a recent memory flashed into his mind of sitting outside this same bishop's office, with Jeanette at his side, listening to Twila Haskins announce that she wanted a cancellation of sealing from her Puritan ancestors. What had Jeanette said? Letting the injured party talk was like lancing the wound; eventually, the real reasons for the anger would come out. "Tell me more," he invited.

For the next half hour, the lanced wound flowed freely. Andrew listened intently, hoping that his counselors could handle the backlog of interviews that he wasn't holding. The bottom line, he decided as Marti's tirade began to ebb, was that she loved Pete deeply but had grown impatient with his reluctance to join the Church and work toward a temple marriage. She had tried to give him the time he seemed to need to commit himself to the gospel, but his vague excuse that he wanted to wait until he was more worthy of baptism had grown thin. She had decided that major scare tactics were the only solution.

"But it's got to be absolutely confidential. You can't mention any of this to anyone else—not to your counselors or your Relief Society president. And especially not to your wife, because she's Gina's friend."

Andrew knew perfectly well what the obligations of a bishop were, but he objected to Marti's assumption that Jeanette would immediately retell the whole story to Gina. His thoughts must have shown clearly on his face, because she continued. "I know Gina. If there's a secret anywhere around, she'll sniff it out and bully your wife into telling it. This is strictly a bluff, and I don't want the kids suffering on account of it."

How she expected to keep a divorce petition and an intimidating lawyer from the knowledge of her children was more than Andrew could envision. Abruptly, he began thumbing through the scriptures, trying to hide the disbelief that she could probably decipher in his face as well as she had read his every other emotion so far.

He turned to the New Testament. Surely the Apostle Paul would have some good advice. But try though he might, Andrew's mind drew a blank when it came to where to find any of these useful passages. This was frustrating! He had aced all his New Testament exams at BYU and had studied the text regularly ever since, but suddenly he couldn't even remember which epistles Paul had written. Finally, he found himself in the fourth chapter of the First Epistle of John, glaring at verse nineteen: "We love him, because he first loved us." It stirred his tired brain, but he didn't really know why. He looked up at Marti, who was still waiting expectantly, and suddenly he saw a new person—a woman ready to risk her security and comfort out of conviction for her new faith, desperate to bring the man she loved to partake of the fruit of life.

"I think you need to cut him some slack," he heard himself say.

She stared at him, speechless.

"I realize how much time you've already given him, but consider how much time the Lord gives each of us to notice the obvious. Let me propose a different strategy." Turning back one page, he read aloud the words of verse seven. "'Beloved, let us love one another: for love is of God; and every one that loveth is born of God, and knoweth God.'" He flipped the page over and read from verse sixteen: "'God is love; and he that dwelleth in love dwelleth in God, and God in him.'" He rounded it off with the words that had first caught his eye. "'We love him, because he first loved us.'"

Marti continued staring. "What does that have to do with anything?" she finally asked.

"Remind Pete of all the reasons he has to love you. People who love can relate to God; His love has a familiar feel to them. That's the way to bring the Spirit of God into his life. Get him thinking about his love for you, and he'll realize that he doesn't want to spend eternity without you. And if you're going where God is, he'll want to be there too. Then he'll be in a frame of mind to feel how much God loves him, and he'll want to show his love in return."

Marti shifted impatiently. "You make it sound so easy," she complained.

"Oh, it isn't easy, but it's worth the trouble. You women are the key to a man's salvation, you know. Most of us are so thickheaded spiritually that we'd never get the idea on our own. Loving a woman puts us in touch with the love of God." He paused, debating whether to add that women need men as well. But Marti looked as if she was pondering pretty deeply, and he realized that she had probably already reached that conclusion.

"I'll tell you what," he suggested. "How about if you give him that slack and show an increase of love for two weeks? If he doesn't start coming around by then, meet with me again—or with your bishop back home—and we'll formulate a new plan."

Marti shot him a suspicious look, as if she suspected that he was simply trying to put her off. Then she drew his open book of scriptures in front of her, turned it around, and began to study the passages on both pages. He waited, giving her plenty of time to consider.

Eventually, she returned the book. "Well, since it's John giving the advice, I guess I'd better take it. If you'd quoted Paul, I'd have blown it off and decked you. That's all I ever hear from my bishop back home."

Mentally, Andrew sighed with relief and thanked the Almighty for the brain freeze about Pauline verses. There was no doubting who was actually in charge around here.

* * *

Pete stood outside by the car, puffing on a cigarette. Marti had been at the store quite a while for someone who just needed to pick up a new tube of mascara. But now she was safely in Gina's house, and he could make that little visit he had been planning since morning. He'd told Vinnie and the women that he wanted to take a look at the neighborhood, so they wouldn't be expecting him back right away. He threw down the cigarette, crushed it with his heel, and walked briskly toward the steeple nearby, hoping that his nerve would hold up.

* * *

With the help of a plate of cookies brought by a thoughtful interviewee, Andrew had managed to recover fairly well from his experience with Marti. Even the visit with the middle-aged, less-active priest who had unexpectedly confessed stealing a set of golf clubs from his former bishop seemed tame by comparison—or perhaps Andrew was merely becoming weary enough to remain more detached. He had sent the man on his way with a carefully composed repentance and restitution plan and was taking a well-deserved minute of rest when Sam Taylor knocked, apologized again, and admitted another of Gina's relatives.

"Bishop McCammon? Pete Locatelli," the man said, offering a hand.

Andrew hadn't needed to be told; the tobacco odor had already preceded Pete to the desk, and it spoke volumes. "Pleased to meet you," he said, praying earnestly that divorce was not on the agenda this time.

"This is strictly confidential, bishop, okay?" Pete clarified as he sat down.

This did nothing to reassure Andrew, but he answered, "Of course."

"Not a word to anyone, especially Marti or Gina. And better not tell Steve or your wife, either. Those Modoni women have built-in radar when it comes to secrets."

"I understand."

"I need to get the names of a real estate agent and your ward employment specialist. And they've got to be good at keeping their mouths shut."

This was a new twist on an old theme. "Uh . . . we haven't called our employment specialist yet." Actually, the bishopric hadn't even discussed that calling yet. "I do know a few realtors, but I don't know that they do any out-of-area work. If you could explain what exactly you need, maybe I could direct you a little better. What kind of job skills do you have?"

"It's a long story," Pete demurred.

Andrew had suspected as much. "Go ahead," he invited.

"Well, I'm . . . kind of a research specialist, I guess. I . . ." He sighed deeply. "I'd better level with you, bishop. I keep track of street gangs for the family business. We're an organized crime ring operating out of Chicago."

Andrew's head started to throb with pain that increased steadily as Pete continued.

"It wasn't my idea for a job. But in my family, it's kind of expected of you, ya know? Marti insisted that I quit when we got married, but it isn't as easy as that. When you know all the family secrets and you don't have a résumé, you can't just hand in your two weeks' notice and move on. So I tried to ease out by tellin' Marti I had switched to a private consultancy firm and tellin' the boys they can't talk business when I'm around, because I don't wanna hafta testify against them sometime. They've been pretty good about it."

"The boys?"

"My dad, my uncles, my cousins, my nephews . . . you get the picture."

Andrew did, unfortunately. His head ached harder.

"I was hopin' that I could kind of wait out the times when they slip and mention business in front of me—let the statute of limitations run out, ya know? Then I could leave the business quietly, and if the law wanted me to testify against any of the boys, I could say honestly that I don't know anything. But somethin' big happened recently, and someone started talkin' about it when I was there. I got out of the room as fast as I could, but I heard who did it and when—I just don't know what. But I know it's big, because the guy's in hot water now, and they told me to get outta state right away. That's why we came early." He paused.

It was apparently Andrew's turn to talk. "You came because your . . . uh . . . family organization wanted you to be unavailable for questioning?"

"Yeah. But the thing is, Marti and the others don't know. At least, I *hope* Marti doesn't know. I dunno if she ever really bought the story about me switching companies. Anyway, I told everyone that my company changed my vacation leave time around on me, so we had to come now. Then I offered to send Gina the message that we'd be here early."

"But you didn't?" asked Andrew, remembering their unexpected arrival.

"Well, I did, but I couldn't risk her writing back and saying she couldn't take us now, ya know? So I altered the e-mail address a little so she wouldn't get it and sent it just before we left. That way I wouldn't have to lie about sending it."

"Ah."

"But there's more. We're not goin' back. Well, maybe Vinnie and Cat and their kids are, but Marti and me and our kids are stayin' here. They don't know that yet, either. The boys don't wanna hafta kill me, ya know, 'cause I'm family, so they want me out of touch. They figured no one'd think of lookin' here. So they packed up all our stuff and put it in storage right after we left, and they sold the place for me. We're living off the proceeds. So I gotta find work and a new place right away."

He paused again. Andrew wanted nothing more than to crawl under his desk, curl up on the floor, and let his head pound freely until this guy left. For a wild moment, he clung to the notion that this was Pete's idea of a great practical joke, but a look into his eyes put that hope to rest. What he saw was a man who was desperate to save his family from perils that they couldn't even imagine. And given his background, he was going to have a tougher time of it than most. Andrew moistened dry lips and forced himself to speak.

"Finding a place to live shouldn't be too hard, but unless you got a tremendous amount in cash from the sale of your old home, you might have trouble buying a house without a job."

Pete shrugged. "We got enough for a down and the first few payments, but we gotta budget it till I find work, ya know?" His hand groped at his sagging shirt pocket. "And another thing, bishop. Marti wants me to join the Church. I do want to—have wanted to from the first time the missionaries came by. They're what I want my son to be like and my daughter to marry. I've been prayin' for a way to get out of the family business so I can join, and this could be it. But I gotta quit smoking, and I haven't been able to do that in ten years of trying. Nicotine gum, nicotine patches, hypnosis, acupuncture—I've tried it all. Nothin' helps. And what with getting away from Chicago and keeping all this stuff from Marti, I'm a nervous wreck, smokin' four packs a day."

Andrew could sympathize, although in the present circumstances, he personally would have preferred a whiff of laughing gas to a cigarette. "Well, let's take first things first. You need to tell your wife."

Pete went rigid. "No way! Not till everything's settled. If I tell her I lied about leavin' the business and we're homeless and penniless because of it, the boys won't have to worry about killin' me; she'll do it for them."

"But how are you going to look for a house without her?"

"Not a problem. I know what she likes, and she could make the city dump into a home."

"So you expect to be gone for hours on end in a strange town with someone she's never met, and she won't wonder why?"

"Well," Pete admitted reluctantly, "there is that."

Eventually, the two of them compromised on looking for work for Pete. Research seemed as likely as field as any, so Andrew agreed to supply lists of possible jobs garnered from the nearest LDS employment center. "Maybe you can search them on a computer at Gina's. You could use it to get a résumé ready, too."

"Not a chance. Gina's got every computer in the house going on family history. The kids can't even squeeze in a video game. And that's the surest way to tip Marti off that something's up."

"Can't we let Steve in on this? He's good at being discreet."

"Out of the question."

Andrew sighed. "I'll loan you my laptop. You can access the Internet from my home wireless if you promise to use it only for researching jobs."

"I promise."

"And ways to quit smoking."

"I tell you, I've tried 'em all!"

"Not all, or you wouldn't still be smoking."

"Can't I tackle these things one at a time?"

"The faster you take them on, the sooner you'll be ready to tell your wife and children. This will be a big change for them, and they deserve some adjustment time. And not smoking isn't exactly a full-time occupation in itself. You'll have two free hands and lots of time to fill."

Pete felt his empty shirt pocket and sighed. "Okay."

* * *

As he stepped out of the deserted meetinghouse into the night, Andrew felt at least a foot shorter from the weight of the problems heaped onto his shoulders. Heaviest of all weighed the secrets that the Locatellis had shared with him. He lifted his face toward the impassive heavens. *What's going on here?* he demanded. *These people aren't even in my ward! Where's their bishop when I need him?*

No response.

Andrew trudged homeward. As the night air stirred gently around him, his temper began to cool, and a wordless apology formed in his mind. This was not God's fault. People made choices, some of which were bound to be bad, and they would suffer and learn from the consequences. If Andrew McCammon weren't in the middle of this hornet's nest, someone else would have to be. *Father,* he thought more humbly, *is this really within my calling?*

Peace washed through him. Well, at least Someone was listening. Encouraged, he thought, *What should I do about it?*

Silence and more peace.

Andrew grappled for a moment with his masculine instinct

to fix this problem and be done with it. Then he relaxed. If the Lord had granted him peace for now, it was enough, he concluded. Still, he wished he could know how it would end.

He glanced upward at the silent heavens. The stars spread across them glimmered slightly.

Ah, well, he thought. *At least I have Jeanette to go home to.* And at the thought, he could feel a spring come into his step.

CHAPTER 6
Enlisting the Living

It was the sleepy time of the afternoon, and several patrons were nodding off in front of their computer screens. Jeanette, fully alert, was buried deep in the 1920 census when her cell phone rang. As the tune to the first movement of Mozart's Fortieth Symphony blared out in the quiet room, she jumped, dove into her bag, drew out the noisy little machine, and flipped it open as she headed for the nearest door.

"Hello," she said breathlessly. "No, just startled me a bit. Hearing from handsome men named Andrew McCammon never disturbs me . . . Still nothing conclusive, but I'm finding lots of documentation . . . Yes, I got the test kit to Fiona, and she's sending it to a company that promises results within ten months. That's the best she could find." She listened intently for a full minute. "All the youth in the ward? How many is that? . . . I'll check the schedule and call you right back . . . Love you too, dear. Bye."

Sure enough, that evening from six thirty on, the family history center was scheduled for the youth of the Twenty-second Ward. Jeanette wondered in passing why neither of the outgoing presidencies of the Young Men and Young Women had alerted her to this activity, seeing as she was supposed to teach it. It was, in fact, the incoming Young Women president who had phoned Andrew minutes ago to tell *him* what was planned. Jeanette shook her head ruefully. It would apparently take a while for the ward members to get used to communicating with each other directly again.

She returned to the hall and dialed Andrew. "Yes, it's still on . . . I wasn't, but I can be ready. Have they been asked to bring anything with them? . . . No problem. I have my laptop with the demo files, and if they get bored, I can always tap dance . . . No, not really, honey—it's just a figure of speech."

The conversation grew more serious as the topic turned to dinner. Jeanette had put a casserole in the oven on timed-bake before leaving for the family history center, but she wanted to be home at dinnertime to serve it. Andrew adamantly refused; she would need the time to prepare for the evening's activity, he insisted, and he and Mark were practiced bachelors who could set a table and put away any leftovers. Eventually Jeanette capitulated, on condition that neither Andrew nor Mark bring her dinner at the center. "Food's not allowed, and I never get hungry while I'm researching. Call it a genealogical diet plan . . . See you after the interviews tonight, then. Bye, darling."

She sighed as she switched the phone to vibrate and slipped it into her pocket. Her main reason for wanting to go home was not to dish out food but to see the light in Andrew's eyes as he looked at her, to feel the reassuring warmth of his arms around her. Their whirlwind courtship, wedding, and honeymoon hadn't yet had time to mellow into the long-term confidence of a marriage, and she missed him every minute. It still seemed too good to be true that she, Jeanette Parkinson, a confirmed old maid for so many years, had become the wife of so wonderful a man as Andrew McCammon. And, she had to admit, the intrusive idea that his feelings for her might someday cool sent icy trickles of despair down her back.

You're letting your insecurities take control, she scolded herself as she returned to her computer. *Andrew says that he loves you, and he's a man of his word. Stop fueling your fears and get back to work.*

Even so, it took nearly a quarter of an hour for the 1920 census to absorb her again.

* * *

Pete leaned against the car door and looked longingly through the window at the half-empty carton of cigarettes. He hadn't been totally honest with the bishop. There was one method of giving up smoking that he hadn't yet tried: the cold-turkey approach. He was trying it now and failing miserably. He fumbled in his pockets for the car keys but pulled his hands out empty. Looking around frantically for some sort of diversion, he found himself staring at a beautiful formation of white clouds, from behind which the sun was streaming in all directions. "God, are you there?" he asked tentatively. "If there's some way to stop this craving, I sure wish you'd show it to me. I'm doing the best I can, ya know."

"Come here," called a voice from nowhere.

Pete caught hold of the side mirror for balance. He hadn't expected such a direct response. It seemed a very young voice for the Being who had created heaven and earth.

It spoke again. "Uncle Pete, over here."

This time he pinpointed the source: a massive broadleaf tree at the back of Gina's house. Its thick, spreading branches seemed to bear some sort of huge wooden box with openings in it. Through the opening nearest him, Marti's nephew Jake was waving his arm. "Come on," he called again. Pete's son, Gianni, joined Jake at the window and beckoned as well.

Pete stared for a moment, then shrugged and ambled on back. When he had reached the foot of the tree, he stopped and peered upward some twenty feet to the wooden structure. "What's this thing?" he asked.

"Our tree house. Dad made it for us," Jake said. "Come on up and see."

"Is it safe?"

"I dunno, but it's sure cool," Gianni replied. "Come on, Dad."

Pete looked in vain for a staircase. "How'd you get up?"

"We climbed the tree," Jake explained.

"It's easy," Gianni chimed in.

"For you, maybe."

"All right, hold on a second." Jake disappeared briefly, then he reappeared with a bundle of rope in his arms. "Stand back," he ordered as he let it fall.

It unrolled into a rope ladder with wooden rungs. "Mom had Dad make this for us in case Hannah got too scared to climb down."

Pete didn't particularly want to admit that he was too scared to climb up, so he grabbed hold of the ropes and began his ascent. The ladder twisted and turned like a live serpent trying to throw him off as he wrestled his way up eight rungs. Stopping for breath, he looked down. The distance to the ground was minimal, compared with that from his seventeenth-story office at the family business. What bothered him was how little there was between him and a hard landing.

"Don't look down," warned a small voice from above. The boys had disappeared; in their place, a dark-haired girl with very blue eyes looked solemnly down at him. "Never look where you don't want to go. Dad told me that."

There was no turning back with those eyes on him. He took a deep breath—triggering his smoker's cough—and struggled up the remaining rungs. With a hand on the side of the opening, he should have felt safer, but he wasn't surprised to find that he didn't. He hesitated, trying to figure out how to let go of the ladder with his other hand without plummeting down.

"Just pretend it isn't moving," the blue-eyed girl advised.

Gritting his teeth, Pete transferred his grip to the wood of the treehouse. Amazingly, the advice worked. With two feet firmly on a solid surface again, he felt almost human. He was not in any hurry to go down, though.

"I'm Hannah," said the girl. "You're Gianni's dad, aren't you?"

"Yep."

"Dad, look at this!" Gianni exclaimed, brandishing a basket with a rope tied to its handle. "Jake's dad made an elevator for the treehouse. It won't carry people, but you can put books and bedding and stuff in it. Jake says he's stayed up here all night sometimes, reading and watching the stars."

"Hmmm." Pete began a cautious inspection of the premises. It seemed sturdy enough, even for an adult, and was spacious enough for the four of them—though two more would have made things crowded. Windows opened in every wall, presenting a bird's-eye view of the neighboring yards. "Nice place," he observed.

"You can come up and play whenever you like," Hannah offered graciously. "Can't he, Jake?"

"Sure, Hannah," Jake answered, clearly without having heard a word of what she had said. "See that blue tower thing over there, Gianni? That's the new waterslide at the swimming pool. We oughta go there, too. And there's an awesome lazy river to float on."

While Jake went on pointing out the sights, Pete sat on the floor, leaned his back against the wall, coughed, and felt his empty shirt pocket. *If the boys could see me now!* he thought mournfully. *Out on a limb, surrounded by munchkins, dying for a smoke.*

Hannah regarded him soberly. "Mom says that you cough because you smoke."

"Your mom's right," Pete conceded.

"Smoking's bad for people," Hannah warned him.

"Yeah, it's bad," Pete agreed, coughing again.

"If you know it's bad, you should stop."

"So they tell me."

"Why don't you?"

Effectively backed into a corner, Pete saw no sense in trying to rationalize his behavior. "'Cause it ain't as easy as some people think."

Hannah blinked thoughtfully as Pete's hand strayed again to his shirt pocket. "I guess it's like when I tried to stop sucking my thumb," she ventured.

"Could be," Pete grunted.

They sat in silence for a moment. Pete's hand moved automatically to his pocket again. He growled irritably, tucked it under his leg, and pressed it hard to the plank flooring.

Hannah gazed steadily at him. "Would you like to hear how I quit sucking my thumb?" she asked.

Any way Pete looked at it, this was going to be one long summer. He slumped against the wall. "Sure, kid," he invited. "Tell me how you quit sucking your thumb."

* * *

Arriving home to an empty, still house was not pleasant, Andrew reflected as he removed the casserole from the oven and placed it on the stove top. It was probably good that he had been able to make his stop at LDS Employment on Pete's behalf without having to make excuses for his late arrival home. But finding Jeanette ready with dinner had been the high point of each day ever since her house had burned down, leaving her a refugee in the household of Gina, a Relief Society president with huge issues on the subject of charity. His house had become Jeanette's daytime haven, and she had rapidly become the new light of his life. He wished for the thousandth time that circumstances had allowed them a longer honeymoon. They would have to take it in installments over the next few years.

Mark's arrival in a gloomy mood underscored the bleakness of the surroundings. The two of them ate quickly and commiserated briefly over Mark's broken engagement before it was time for Mark to depart for his Wednesday-night class. Andrew was preparing to walk to the meetinghouse and another evening of interviews when Chief Ridley's trademark knock sounded at the door.

"Hey, Mr. McCammon, I need your help again," he announced.

Andrew stood aside to allow him to come in, but the chief must have sensed the starkness of the home in Jeanette's absence, because he remained on the porch. "Got a problem with the dead guy's family. Well, not really *them,* I guess—just I've got no place to put 'em. They have no relatives in the area and no money, our department budget's stretched to the max, and we're gettin' nowhere with government services. The homeless shelter is full to overflowing, and so's the safe house for abuse cases. My wife's taken a liking to them, and she's all for puttin' them up ourselves. Kind of outside the norm, I guess, but I feel good enough about these folks that I'm willing. Trouble is, my house is too small while my family's home. I considered sendin' the girls to Tif's, but things are pretty chaotic there right now, and I can't ask her to host 'em in her present state. So I was wondering if someone'd be willing to take in four of my daughters for a week or so."

The last thing Andrew wanted was a houseful of strange girls to witness the beginning of his new married life. "Well, I—"

"We'll keep Bethany with us, of course. She's the youngest one, see, only nine. And the third oldest—Steffany's her name—said she might already have a place. Her best friend from school's been wanting her to come for a sleepover. Tawni Taylor."

Tawni was a ward member—Sam Taylor's daughter, in fact. Andrew realized suddenly that Steffany must be "Stef," the sandy-haired girl, a recent convert, whom Tawni shepherded around everywhere. And Bishop Farr had told him that another of the Ridley girls had joined the Church too. Well, like it or not, this was his responsibility—and the ward's. But it probably wouldn't do to get Gina involved; she had problems of her own, whether she knew it or not. "I think we can take care of it, chief. What are your other daughters' names, and how old are they?"

"Brittany, Mellany, and Tammany. Brit's eighteen, Mel's fourteen, and Tam's twelve."

It took a few minutes to get the four "-any"s straightened out and their ages recorded. Andrew promised to get back with Chief Ridley by eight that evening with arrangements, then set off for the meetinghouse at a fast walk, phoning Jeanette as he went.

"Hi, honey. I've got another minor catastrophe . . . You *specialize* in them? I definitely married the right woman, then. Here it is." Briefly he outlined the situation and asked her to solicit volunteer hostesses from among the young women at the activity that evening. Her response was all confidence and optimism. There was time for a very few words of love and the promise of a Friday-night date before he entered the meetinghouse and greeted the first of the evening's interviewees.

* * *

Jeanette couldn't have said when the idea occurred to her or why. Maybe it was the bright, unexpectedly intelligent expressions on the young faces before her. Maybe it was the eagerness with which they volunteered to take in the temporarily homeless Ridley girls, regardless of which of them was actually a Church member, and the enthusiasm with which they carried their way with their parents in a flurry of cell-phone calls. ("Mom, think of the missionary opportunity!" Jeanette overheard from one Beehive girl.) After the arrangements had been finalized, Jake and his sister Sarah took the floor for a few minutes to introduce their cousins from Chicago, who had arrived diffident but were warming nicely to the welcome being given them. By the time

Jeanette arose to present the lesson, she had already decided to toss her carefully prepared plan and take a totally different tack.

"How many of you young people here remember Mark McCammon?" she asked.

A forest of hands went up.

"Had any of you heard that he was engaged?"

A chorus of "ooh"s and well-wishes swept the room, especially from the girls.

"That's good of you all, but I'm sorry to report that the engagement is off."

A new chorus of "aww"s and groans ensued. Encouraged, Jeanette outlined what had happened, noticing the quick sympathy in the faces of the young people as she described the distressed state of mind of the ill-fated couple. "Would you like to change things for them if you could?"

Assured by nods that they would, Jeanette asserted warmly, "Here's where family history research might help us out." With a few keystrokes on her laptop computer, she produced on a projection screen the pedigree of Irene Jarvis's purported blood lineage. "I've entered here the lineage for several generations," she began and paused, wondering how far back the line should be investigated. Logically, it made more sense to deal with only the latest generations, but for some reason, the family of Thomas and Mary Barnes stood out in her mind. *It couldn't* hurt *to go back that far,* she decided. *The point for them is the exercise, after all.*

"Here's what we'll do," she continued aloud. "Let's divide into groups, and I'll assign each group a family to research. Your objective is to try to prove that what appears here"— she tapped the projection screen—"is wrong by using the records of the time. That means the census, vital records indexes, journals— anything you can find. First, let me show you how the databases work and what to watch for as you search them."

Jeanette had never taught a more attentive audience. It amazed her to see how much difference it made when her students began with a sense of purpose rather than merely duty. She fielded dozens of questions, all of them intelligent and intense. Then she provided each team with a printed report of its assigned family group. For good measure, she included the families of each of Susan's mother's siblings. Because of privacy laws, she didn't assign them anyone from Susan's own generation; she had already spent the afternoon investigating those herself and had found precious little. Finally, she let the young people take control of the computers.

They descended on the problem with an acuity that amazed her. For a while, she and the other center volunteers moved from group to group, helping with analysis of the families, suggesting strategies, and interpreting cryptic handwriting in the scanned images on the computer screens. Then, as prearranged with Andrew, she withdrew to the hallway and telephoned him with the names and phone numbers of the families who had consented to host the Ridley girls. Hearing from him that she was magnificent didn't quite make up for missing dinner with him, but it came close.

"It's quite a compliment Chief Ridley is paying to our ward members, isn't it? Imagine him sending his daughters to stay with a group of comparative strangers . . . Hmm. I guess he *is* in a position to run background checks on any of us, isn't he? Well, even if he did, I wouldn't blame him. With six daughters, I'd be protective, too . . . Oh, it's going really well. I'll tell you all about it tonight . . . I love you too, sweetheart. See you soon."

Work on Irene Jarvis's supposed blood lineage proceeded rapidly. Even though the young people were inexperienced, they brought forward a quantity of records that would have taken Jeanette weeks to amass. Jeanette accepted them all with high praise for the researchers, although she could tell at a glance that many of them were not reliable and none of them disproved Irene's relationship to Susan. This was the nature of family history research, after all: a thousand mundane disappointments for every thrilling discovery. She filed them away into manila folders—one per family group—to study later. As she analyzed and synthesized the information, she would look for any clues or discrepancies that could help her reconstruct the complete scenario behind Irene's birth and adoption.

By eight thirty, though, enthusiasm was waning. Jeanette wisely called a halt and directed the young people to another room well supplied with doughnuts and milk, provided incognito by the incoming presidencies. Following a closing prayer and blessing on the roomful of nearly nutritionless calories, she busied herself pouring milk. The conversation among the youth at first concerned research discoveries and was rather subdued. Fueled by sugar, it quickly turned to the topic of summer activities and grew more boisterous. By the time they were beginning to leave, Jeanette's head was ringing with their chatter. She was in the process of dividing up the leftover refreshments among those who remained when a girl in her midteens—a uniquely quiet one—tugged at her sleeve.

"Could I get a copy of the family group sheet from Parowan, please?" the girl asked.

Jeanette turned too suddenly, and a wave of dizziness swept over her. "Uh . . . sorry, which one?"

"From Parowan. My grandparents lived there."

Jeanette quickly grabbed a doughnut and bit into it in an unsuccessful attempt to stave off another attack of dizziness. "You're Cyndi Blake, aren't you?" she asked as she seized the edge of the refreshment table in a death grip. "I'll tell you what: go ahead and take the group sheet from the manila folder. I'll print out another one later."

The girl nodded and left, heading toward the computer room. Jeanette sank into a chair, finished her doughnut, and poured herself a drink of milk for good measure. Still slightly dazed, she smiled vacuously as the remaining youth squabbled airily over the spoils. When at last they departed with them, she had energy for little more than to gather up her stack of manila folders, help close the center, and drive home.

Fortified by a small portion of warmed-up casserole, Jeanette was debating whether to start examining the documents that night when Mark arrived in a black mood. "A girl in the class got engaged last night. It was totally disgusting how she flashed that ring around. The way she twittered on and on about her *fiancé*"—laying heavy emphasis on the despised word—"just about made me hurl. Girls that giddy shouldn't be allowed to get married." Clearly, this was no time to spread out the family group sheets. Jeanette stirred up a pot of hot chocolate and spent the evening diverting Mark's thoughts to more neutral ground. By the time he retired to bed, she was exhausted again.

She had planned to prepare the bedroom for Andrew as before, with candlelight, fragrance, and a welcoming bed. But before she could even make a move in that direction, the front door opened and he entered, sniffing. "I smell hot chocolate. Is there any left for a worn-out old fellow like me?"

Jeanette suddenly felt energy flow into her tired body. "Chocolate is the sure cure for anything, and fellows like you get a fresh pot in the flavor of their choice," she answered, going to him and wrapping her arms around his neck.

"'If chocolate be the food of love, brew on,'" he misquoted with a breathtaking smile. Then he delayed the fulfillment of his own request with several lengthy kisses.

CHAPTER 7
Investigating the Dead

At breakfast the next morning, the three McCammons updated their schedules.

"Jeanette, would you be willing to contact the host families for the Ridley girls to be sure that all is going well? Between work and interviews, I'm afraid that no one in the bishopric can spare the time to do it," Andrew began apologetically.

"No problem," Jeanette replied, happy to relieve some stress from Andrew's hectic week. "I can do that before I meet Gina and her cousins at the Family History Library in Salt Lake City. I'm really sorry about two timed-bake dinners in a row, but I'll try to be home to serve it up. What would you two like?"

"It's up to Dad," Mark said dully as he moved the half-eaten breakfast around on his plate. "I'm heading back to my own apartment after work."

Andrew and Jeanette stared at him silently for a moment, then they spoke simultaneously.

"Are you sure you're ready to be alone?"

"Won't you stay longer? We love having you."

Mark gave what might have been a very strained half smile. "I need to stop imposing on you and face my problems like a man."

Another pause. Again, Jeanette and Andrew broke it in the same instant.

"But you aren't imposing on us!"

"This will always be a home to you, son."

Mark's fleeting smile was a little more genuine this time. "This is like old times, Dad. You and Mom always used to try to talk at the same time when you were worried about us." Then he turned somber again. "It isn't only that, I guess. The Jarvises will be in the neighborhood a lot, translating for the police chief and that Slovenian family. I'm just afraid of running into them. It would be embarrassing to start bawling in front of them."

"You're not going to nurse a grudge, are you, Mark?" Andrew asked.

"I'm trying not to, but it isn't easy," he answered frankly. "My mind knows that they're not at fault, but my heart's pretty torn up right now. I'd rather lie low somewhere so that I don't say or do anything we'll all regret later on."

Jeanette could understand completely but wondered if she had the right to say so. Mark was, after all, Andrew's son. Andrew and Susan's.

Andrew took a deep breath. "Handle it as you see fit, but please don't shut us out. If you need us, we'll come to your place. I'll drop-kick any number of interviews if you say the word."

"And I'll tell Gina that I can't make it today," Jeanette interjected.

This time Mark gave an honest-to-goodness smile, though it faded rapidly. "Sister Roylance would have a fit, Nan. But don't worry. I'll be at work all day and at my night class most of the evening, and Fio will probably camp on my doorstep if she finds out I'm not here."

Fiona was a nurse-practitioner and an excellent grief counselor, as Jeanette knew from firsthand experience. She made a mental note to phone her stepdaughter as soon as Mark left for work. She could tell from the look in Andrew's eyes as he gazed at her that he had the same idea. But all he said was, "Never mind fixing another dinner, dear. I can microwave some leftovers before I head to the church. I suspect that Gina is going to need your help, so stay as long as you need to. They'll probably need someone to show them where to eat in Salt Lake. With that curfew of hers, Gina probably doesn't know the city very well."

Part of Jeanette felt relieved that her new husband was so very understanding. But another part felt hurt that she was so expendable in his life. She couldn't picture Susan leaving at a moment of family crisis. *How would Susan have told Gina no?* she wondered. But it didn't really matter. She would concentrate on following Andrew's instructions and try to ignore the shadow of Susan across her marriage.

* * *

Jeanette had seemed rather subdued, Andrew mused as he drove to work. It might have been that she was preoccupied with the day of research to come. Andrew knew that besides helping with Gina's research, Jeanette planned to examine the records of Susan's troublesome family line for a flaw that might help Mark. That was enough of an agenda for one day to subdue even the most ardent researcher. Privately, he hoped that she had no more to contend with than that.

He sighed. Maybe it was his natural pessimism speaking, but he was certain that the conflicting secrets of Pete and Marti were destined to collide. When they did, he anticipated a display of emotional fireworks that would attract the awestricken notice of everyone within a ten-mile radius. He longed to warn Gina and Steve, but he had solemn promises to keep—promises binding enough that he could not even alert Jeanette to the possibilities. The thought that she might end up in the midst of the fray did not sit well with his instincts as husband and knight in shining armor. But Gina would be far worse off, because her familial hopes and loyalties would be at risk. And once the other two cousins became involved—as they undoubtedly would—it would be utter mayhem. Even Steve, the voice of reason, might not be able to calm those troubled waters. Gina's remark about wanting Jeanette for a counselor had been a huge admission of how much the brusque Italian-American woman had come to depend on her friend's quiet steadiness. Jeanette's presence at such a time, much though it unnerved him, might mean the difference between Gina withstanding the crisis or going into total meltdown.

He sighed again. Jeanette's insistence that she needed to spend breakfast with him and Mark had kept her from joining Gina's family party on the commuter rail that morning. But it was only a matter of time, he felt sure, until the blowup came.

His project at work that day was of the irksome variety that bored him to death even while it demanded his full attention. Except during his lunch break, he had little time to speculate on how Jeanette's day was going, how Mark was faring, or what the fate of the Locatellis might be. He had even less time to spare for the Jarvises and the Slovenian family. Thus, finding Chief Ridley on his doorstep upon arriving home was an unexpected shock. His first concern was that something might have happened to one of the daughters being hosted by the ward.

"Naw, nothing like that," the chief reassured him when he asked. "The girls are havin' the time of their lives. And the families they're stayin' with are as law-abiding as they come. Your people are the only ones I'd trust with 'em. It's the other thing I'm here about—the Slovenlyan folks. That Jarvis couple took 'em right under their wings and got their whole story."

As he was talking, Andrew got the front door open and motioned for the chief to precede him into the house. Once inside, he paused and looked around. "Where's the missus?"

"She's helping a friend entertain some relatives from out of town," Andrew replied, squelching his urge to ask what business it was of the chief's.

"Mmm. I was hopin' to enlist her help too. She's got a head on her shoulders. Well, I'll fill you in and you can pass the word to her. After the last time we had to break up a domestic dispute at the Slovenlyans' place, it seems the stiff got detox help for his alcohol problem. The family says he was bone-dry for six weeks, but he'd already lost a buncha jobs in the area, see, and no one else wanted to take a chance on him. So he went to Vegas looking for work. His widow says he phoned from there and said he'd found a good job—sent money and said he'd drive up and get 'em. Later he phoned and said he'd had car trouble, so they had to take the bus. He arranged to meet 'em at a bus station in Vegas. They went, but he never showed. Some charity group down there took them in just to keep 'em off the streets. They never heard a word from anyone about him till my detective showed up.

"The family had dates for when they heard from him and when they moved, and so far it all checks out. They swear there was no grave in the backyard when they left. I reviewed my records on the case and got the dates for when that vacuum-skulled woman who moved in after them started phoning about the dog and when we dug the stiff up. What I don't have yet is the record of the phone calls the family got—we've subpoenaed it, but it takes a while—and a date when the grave first appeared. I'm assuming that whoever dug it didn't take the trouble to plant it over with weeds, see, so there must've been a bare patch back there for a while. I need to know who might've been living near enough by to notice it. The address is 478 North 150 West."

Thanks to the recent boundary change, Andrew knew exactly where the house was and could supply the names of the nearest neighbors. It was, he realized with a pang, the vacant place three houses away and around the corner from the Roylance home, as if Gina needed any more hassles to cope with right now. Fortunately, Chief Ridley seemed to think that the Roylances lived too far away to have seen or heard anything useful. "We'll question them if we run out of other leads, but we'll start with the folks next door and across the back fence."

Andrew could not guarantee that these neighbors had even been living there when the incident had occurred, but the chief seemed unconcerned. "It's a place to start. We aren't racin' the clock on this one, though it'll be nice to resolve it cleanly for the sake of the family."

By the time Chief Ridley left, Andrew had time to half-warm a helping of casserole, swallow it practically without chewing it, and grab a banana for the road. He made it to the meetinghouse with fifteen seconds to spare before his first interview and no time to check in with either Jeanette or Mark.

* * *

Jeanette's day flew by. Because the Modoni family—Gina's maternal line—had come to America during an era of increasingly good record keeping, Jeanette was able to spend most of the day on the U.S. and Canada floor, alternately helping Gina and her cousins comb the Chicago records and making minuscule amounts of progress in her own research on Susan's line. Marti caught on to the research process quickly, and Cat rapidly proved herself competent at everything except the nineteenth-century handwriting. Vinnie lagged behind in research and deciphering skills, but he was a genius at finding his way through computer databases. He also made himself useful by retrieving and refiling microfilms. Pete performed some skilled and very fruitful Internet searches but became more fractious as the day went on. He frequently excused himself for breaks of about a quarter of an hour.

"He's stashed his death sticks in a locker downstairs," Gina muttered to Jeanette as Pete left yet again. "The tobacco ash will be knee-deep on the sidewalk outside by the time we leave. The man's a mobile contamination station."

Jeanette couldn't help but sympathize with him. Her own father had indulged his taste for cola for decades before giving it up at his doctor's insistence. The weeks that he had spent wandering aimlessly through the house licking his dry lips were still etched in her memory. "Breaking an addiction can be a hard thing," she offered in his defense.

"I only wish he were *trying* to break it," Gina replied curtly.

To conserve precious research time, the family had opted for a single midafternoon meal. Jeanette conducted them on the two-block walk to a popular Italian-themed restaurant and listened with alternating amazement and amusement as the cousins compared research findings, freely criticized each other's abilities, and argued volubly over memories of family heritage that had long been blurred by time before any of them was born.

"I don't *care* what you say, Pete—dearest—I *know* that Aunt Lucia said her grandparents came from Lecce," insisted Marti, pounding the table emphatically. The contrast between the dulcet tone of endearment and the passionately expressed remainder of the sentence was striking, but only Pete and Jeanette seemed to notice it.

"Aunt Lucia was crazy as a loon by the time you turned two," Vinnie retorted. "Uncle Paolo said they came from Taranto."

"And who said Uncle Paolo wasn't even crazier?" Gina rejoined sharply. "He's the one who claimed that the lineage went back to Brindisi in the eighteenth century. Ever wonder how he knew so much about it when he spent most of his youth in Bari with his Capitano cousins? He wouldn't know Brindisi if it bit him on the leg."

"Well, don't blame *me*," Cat remonstrated. "*My* people came from Caserta."

"Mine came from Palermo," growled Pete, groping at his empty shirt pocket.

"More's the pity," snapped Marti. Then, as an afterthought, she added tenderly, "sweetie."

Pete glared at her in irritated confusion. Then he sat heavily on both his hands.

Jeanette ate faster and said nothing.

Once inside the library's front doors, Pete detached himself from the group of still-wrangling adults and headed for the locker area on the main floor. As the rest of the Modoni clan waited at the elevators, scrabbling through a steady stream of names of senile elderly relatives and towns in southern Italy, Jeanette noticed Pete walking back out the front door with a small collapsible cooler in his hand. She had only an instant to wonder what sort of tobacco needed refrigeration before Gina reclaimed her attention with a demand for information about records that had survived the 1871 Chicago fire. She was still combing her memory for details when the elevator arrived.

Half an hour later, the Modoni cousins had found enough verification in the United States to satisfy them all and were ready to cross the ocean to Italy. Jeanette escorted them down two levels to the international floor and, leaving them in the hands of an Italian research consultant, gratefully headed back upstairs to tackle her own research problems. Consulting a meticulously prioritized list, she located and photocopied records at top speed without attempting to synthesize her findings. That could be done at home, and she might not have another chance to return to Salt Lake City for several weeks. She was just rewinding the last microfilm indicated on the portion of her list labeled "Must Have; Available Only in Salt Lake" when Gina appeared at her shoulder.

"We need help. The place closes in half an hour, and we've got four films to search. Vinnie and Cat can't read the writing, and Pete keeps trying to smoke himself to death. Come on."

Jeanette cast longing eyes at the next column of her list, labeled "Could Be Useful; Only in Salt Lake" and nodded. She could order microfilms or make time to come back if she had to. For the visiting Modonis, this research opportunity might be their one and only. Hastily gathering up her papers, she followed Gina to the elevator.

They finished the last films with the overhead lights switched on full and library personnel breathing down their necks. A headlong dash and complete disregard of the crosswalk signals brought them to the light-rail stop seconds before the train was ready to pull out. They made it on board only because a kindly passenger held the door open for them. After transferring to the commuter rail, the Modoni cousins spent the trip home alternately praising and condemning their forebears for the paper trail they had or had not left. Jeanette heard just enough to indicate that Aunt Lucia's recollections had triumphed over Uncle Paolo's before she tuned out to telephone Fiona.

She and Spencer, her husband, were still at Mark's apartment. Mark was, as Fiona expressed it, "down but stable." Jeanette regretted that she couldn't provide him with any good news. When the call was finished, she debated phoning Andrew but decided against interrupting any interviews. She would be at home before he finished the rigorous schedule his executive secretary had laid out for him. Absently, she watched Pete feel his empty shirt pocket, fiddle briefly with the cooler in his hand, and subside with a gloomy sigh. If he could endure the wait, so could she.

* * *

Andrew must have looked as exhausted as he felt when he stepped in the front door, because Jeanette immediately looked very self-conscious. She had obviously worked to create a romantic mood, with soft lighting and the languorous strains of Beethoven's Sixth Symphony, already into its second movement, playing in the background. He quickly drew on his last reserves of energy and poured them into a long, appreciative kiss. It wasn't a difficult task at all, he found.

"All that's missing are a few fauns, centaurs, unicorns, and winged horses," he observed, plunking gratefully onto a chair by the table.

"This isn't exactly the fruit of the vine," Jeanette demurred as she offered him a cup of aromatic almond hot chocolate.

"It's ambrosia," he assured her. "*Fantasia* was always one of my favorite movies. The best part was when Zeus zapped the wine vat with a lightning bolt."

She giggled. "Because it got rid of the wine?"

He smiled boyishly. "Because it was so funny to see Dionysus and his 'mulicorn' getting soused on grape juice that hadn't even fermented."

She laughed with him. "I hadn't thought about that," she admitted. "Being a girl, I was more partial to the calm after the storm."

Andrew finished off his hot chocolate with a yawn. "Well, I'm about ready to do what Zeus did—kick off my sandals and wrap up in a cloud for a nice, long nap." Then he grimaced. "Oh yeah—Chief Ridley stopped by. He wanted me to brief you on what the Jarvises learned from the Slovenian family. I don't know why the chief is certain that genealogy skills make someone an expert in dead bodies."

"I suppose I set him a faulty precedent when I helped him identify the one and locate his hometown," admitted Jeanette. "But, darling"—Andrew took a moment to revel in the sound of that word—"you don't need to brief me tonight. Tomorrow Gina is taking everyone to see some of the local museums, so I'll be free to talk to the Jarvises and get the story from them. Maybe I can work around to the topic of Irene's genealogy. I've wanted an excuse to get more information from her."

"How did the search go?" he asked, trying to hold back another yawn.

She took his hand, led him back to the bedroom, and let him prepare for bed as she described the hectic day with the Modonis and the stack of papers she had yet to examine. Andrew listened to her accounts of Pete's tobacco cooler and Marti's honey-coated barbs and tried to smile, but knowing what he knew made it difficult for him to savor the humor. He hoped that she would attribute his seeming indifference to weariness.

Apparently she did. Following couple prayer, she kissed him briefly and left him to his private prayer while she brushed her teeth and prepared for bed. By the time she'd snuggled in next to him, he was almost asleep.

CHAPTER 8
Unfulfilled Promises

Jeanette got the story of the Slovenian family nearly firsthand. By the time she arrived at the Ridley home, Del and Irene Jarvis were already there and were translating a long list of questions compiled by the chief and his detectives. Chief Ridley interrupted the proceedings long enough to introduce her to the tiny, swarthy-complexioned woman and her even tinier, gray-haired, wizened mother. As the interview continued, Jeanette's eyes were drawn to the two children, a boy of about nine and a girl about six years old. The dark confusion and pain in their eyes completely melted her heart.

Through the Jarvises, the widow told a sorrowful tale. The family had waited six years for permission to come to America and had nearly been denied passage at the last moment when the man sponsoring them had unexpectedly died. The hurriedly impressed second sponsor had done the minimum to help the family adjust before he himself moved to another state. The father and sole breadwinner, though willing to work hard, had lost several jobs within a period of a month due to layoffs.

"That set off the drinking problem," Del explained. "Before that, he'd been the perfect family man, his wife says."

Chief Ridley snorted slightly at this. He clearly believed that perfect family men didn't become drunken wife beaters overnight, alcohol notwithstanding.

Irene Jarvis rose to the deceased man's defense. "He was isolated and terribly depressed," she temporized with the slightest hint of reproach in her voice. "We'll never know what was going through his mind. And he did straighten his life out in the end."

The chief nodded but seemed to remain unconvinced. He had, Jeanette surmised, received a rather negative impression of the man from his officers. She gathered that they had been summoned several times to subdue him during his drunken bouts. However, his family members had obviously loved him and were willing to forgive him all. Personally, she saw no harm—especially now—in giving him the benefit of the doubt.

Her eyes strayed again to the children. They must be devastated to have arrived in America with such high hopes, only to lose their father under such mysterious circumstances. The dark-haired boy sat with his shoulders hunched, as if he had assumed a load of responsibility far too heavy for one so young. The flaxen-haired little girl sat perfectly still, blue eyes wide, clutching what may have been her only toy—a patched rag doll. She looked exactly like a Precious Moments figurine about to burst into tears.

Within minutes, the chief concluded his questions, scribbled a few notes, and called out, "Bethany? You can come in now." Immediately, a dark-haired girl a few years older than the immigrants' daughter darted into the room and warmly hugged the little statue-girl, who seemed to come to life.

"C'mon, Vesna," Bethany said, catching the other girl by the hand, "let's walk our dolls. Amy's already strapped in, and I've got the stroller all ready for Milijana. Tadej," she added, turning to the boy, "you can come as our bodyguard."

Tadej nodded gravely and rose.

Chief Ridley tousled Bethany's hair lovingly as he passed her on his way out of the room. As the children left in their turn, the Jarvises offered to their mother and grandmother what were probably some words of consolation and encouragement. They must not have said the right thing, though, because the younger woman's face contorted into a grief-stricken mask, and she wailed a statement in her native tongue that reduced the older woman to loud sobs.

"Oops," Del muttered.

Irene turned to Jeanette. "She said, 'He promised to meet us.' That's been her refrain ever since we first spoke to her." She sighed. "We can't seem to say anything that helps. None of them has any spiritual training or background, so talking about an afterlife means nothing to them. And Lenka"—she motioned to the younger widow—"is too overcome to try to understand."

Jeanette hesitated, debating inwardly. She knew who could help, but it would mean taking needed support from Mark. Still, she knew what Mark himself would do. "Maybe a professional grief counselor could help," she offered. "Mark's sister, Fiona, is a specialist in that field."

A quick phone call established that Fiona had some free time that afternoon and would be happy to come by.

"Possibly you could help us with another problem," Del said somewhat awkwardly. "The family's being well hosted here by the Ridleys, who've had to farm out their own children to do it. Once the investigation is wrapped up, there's really nowhere these poor folks can go. Is there any way the bishop could—"

"Of course," Jeanette broke in, chiding herself for not having thought of it sooner. "They'll need food, clothing, a place to stay, and job training. Andrew is the obvious person to help with all that. He may already have some ideas in that direction."

While Del chatted with Lenka and her mother to ascertain what plans, if any, they had for their future, Jeanette drew Irene aside. Having just indebted the Jarvises doubly to the McCammon family, she felt relatively confident in approaching

Irene again on the ticklish subject of her birth parentage. However, she received little satisfaction. Instead, with every word Irene uttered, she seemed to bury Jeanette's and Mark's hopes a bit deeper.

"Actually, the lineage was researched. All the sources were detailed on the back of the researcher's family group sheets. I didn't realize at the time that they'd be important, and I didn't have much time or money with me that day, so I didn't photocopy the backs—just the fronts."

Jeanette's heart sank.

"It's possible that the woman who traced the lineage made a mistake," Irene continued. "But she certainly seemed confident about it. She's retired now, but she had researched professionally for years and had some sort of certification or accreditation in United States family history."

Jeanette knew from investigation how competent in research a person had to be to gain accreditation or certification. Her heart sank further.

"There was only one clue available to me when I began the search," Irene went on, taking from her purse a small, needlepoint-covered case. She drew from it a laminated, index card–sized reduction of a typewritten sheet of paper. "This is a letter that my birth mother wrote to me. She gave it to my adoptive parents and asked them to pass it on to me if ever I asked about my birth mother. I read it for the first time when I was about thirteen." She handed it to Jeanette, who gingerly took it.

"Are you sure that you want me to read something so private?" she asked uncertainly.

Irene smiled sadly. "The least I can do for Mark is to explain as fully as possible why we had to withdraw our consent."

Jeanette nodded and began to read. The printing was tiny on the laminated card, but its significance was huge.

Dearest Little One,

I may be unreasonable, but part of me hopes that someday you will become curious about me and will read this letter. I want you to know that it is not because I don't love you that I am giving you away. In fact, although you resulted from a serious mistake in judgment, I love you with all my heart, and at first I was determined to keep you. You, I felt, were one human being whom I could count on to love me as much as I love you.

But when I arrived in Parowan, Cleve and Charlotte persuaded me to put your welfare above my own selfish feelings. They helped me to understand that your life with me would be second-rate. With the little amount of education that I have, I can never hope to earn enough to make your life pleasant and secure or to send you to college. My own future chances of education or marriage would be close to nonexistent. By keeping you, I would condemn both of us to lives of poverty, uncertainty, struggle, and ignorance.

Then they told me about a wonderful couple who love children but have none of their own. These good people could offer you stability, a comfortable home, a bright future, and a great deal of love. Best of all, they would raise you to know and cherish God and to avoid the mistakes I have made. I have prayed to God and know with certainty that they will raise you far better than I can ever hope to do. So I am giving you, my most precious little girl, to these fine people. Please love and honor them, for God Himself has chosen them to be your parents.

> *Someday I hope that you will appreciate how great a sacrifice I am making for your happiness. I love you, and I always will. Good-bye, my angel daughter.*
>
> *L.*

Tears stung Jeanette's eyes as she touched the single initial at the end of the letter. *L,* she thought. *Susan's mother's name was Linda.* By now her heart was resting on the soles of her shoes. Her optimism had evaporated. She was torn between empathy for the teenage mother and grief for Mark's lost hopes, but she could not deny it: all the evidence upheld the conclusion that Irene was right.

Jeanette drove to the family history center and spent the afternoon alternating between dogged research and despairing indecision over how to break this bad news to Andrew and Mark. Anxiously, she searched the records compiled by the ward's young people for anything that might give her a reason to hope, but several restless hours of synthesis merely built a stronger case for Irene's relationship to Susan. On top of everything else, she had misplaced at least one family group sheet and, in searching for it, had managed to set all her other manila folders in total disarray.

Completely frustrated, Jeanette found herself, for the first time in her life, hating family history. *Why am I even bothering?* she asked herself. Angrily, she packed up her manila folders, drove home, and stuck them on a high shelf in a closet where she wouldn't have to look at them. A long soak in a bubble bath restored her to a modest degree of composure, and she decided, for Andrew's sake, to keep the existence of Irene's letter to herself until Monday. Once his first Sunday in charge of the ward was successfully past, she and Andrew would face together the prospect of telling Mark.

* * *

Andrew hurried home with a light heart. It was Friday, and only an hour's worth of interviews awaited him this evening. Then the night was his and Jeanette's. Their session at the temple would be followed by an activity of Andrew's choosing. He had already decided on dessert at Neville's, a gourmet café and bakery built and decorated to resemble a small medieval castle. Next, they would stroll through a nearby park on a stone pathway, roofed by trellises heavily hung with roses, which led to a secluded gazebo beside the river. Susan had found the place enchanting, and he was confident that Jeanette would love it just as much.

Dinner was delicious, though it had to be eaten in haste. Jeanette had already dressed for the evening in a raspberry-colored gown of some light, flowing fabric. She looked fabulous, and Andrew could only bring himself to leave her by recalling that in an hour he would be back.

The interviews proceeded well. No problems reared their ugly heads this evening, and the prospect of a smoothly operating ward on Sunday shone like a welcoming beacon. He was just adding the final names to the list of people to be sustained in sacrament meeting when Sam Taylor tapped at the door, grimaced apologetically at him, and admitted Pete Locatelli.

"Come in, Brother Locatelli." Andrew shook Pete's hand and motioned him to a seat while glancing at the clock on the facing wall. He was ahead of schedule, and all would be well if Pete didn't stay longer than about ten minutes. "I've got a list of Internet job sites for you," he declared, pulling a sheet of paper from his briefcase and handing it across the desk. "How has it been going with the résumé?"

"It's a problem," Pete confessed, taking the job list and folding it nervously into a lopsided wad without even looking at it. "Especially hiding out from the others while I work on it. I found a place, but it's got no electricity, so I gotta work in the daylight on battery. Then I plug your laptop into the car and go drivin' around in the evening to recharge it." He hoisted the case containing Andrew's laptop computer onto the desk.

"Have you been able to prepare a draft?" Andrew asked, opening the case and retrieving the computer.

"Yeah, I guess, but I've got no place to print it."

Andrew located Pete's résumé file and transferred it to his flash drive. "I'll print it out at home for you," he offered, "but let's have a look at it now."

"Naw, wait till it's printed," Pete requested. "I gotta talk to you about something else."

Andrew closed the laptop and returned it to Pete. "What's on your mind?"

"Marti mostly," said Pete glumly. "I think she's up to something."

Andrew tensed. *She must have gotten impatient and started negotiations with a lawyer.*

"She's quit harpin' on me about my smoking," Pete complained, "and it's all of a sudden honey this and sweetie that and deary-dear all over the place."

"And you . . . don't like that?" Andrew tried not to look openly incredulous.

"It's not bad in itself," Pete admitted, "but it isn't like Marti. It's real suspicious—like how the wind dies down right before the storm of the century hits, ya know?"

Andrew sighed inwardly. There was just no pleasing some people. "Well, you might as well enjoy it, especially if you don't think it's going to last. And maybe it will. Have you told your family yet that you'll be staying here?"

"No way!" Pete answered vehemently. "It's all gotta be settled first, ya know? But I been askin' the kids how they like it here. Really casual-like, ya know, so that they don't suspect I got any reason for it. They like it a lot, so I'm bettin' they'll be fine with it."

"Have you asked Marti?"

Pete shook his head vigorously. "I don't dare ask her. She'd find out why and tie my ears in a knot."

Andrew sighed. *Why couldn't every wife be as lovable and understanding as Jeanette?* he wondered. "How are you coming along with quitting smoking?"

Pete groaned. "That's the other thing. I'm tryin' something new, but it's murder, ya know? I dunno if I'll be able to stick it out."

"But consider the rewards if you do," Andrew encouraged him. "What are you trying? I'll be happy to help if I can."

Pete twisted his mouth wryly. "Well, it's kinda . . . weird . . ."

Muffled voices sounded beyond the door to the clerk's office. Pete jerked his head around to face it, fascinated horror in his eyes. "That's Marti. I'd know that holler anywhere. What's she doing here?"

Andrew would have liked to know the same thing. The clock now stood at seven twenty-five, and he should be starting home to meet Jeanette.

"I can't let her find me here!" Pete exclaimed as he rose, panicking. "It'd give the whole game away. I gotta go. Look, bishop, can you meet me later? Maybe at that gas station with the deli in it?"

"Not tonight," Andrew objected automatically. The knob on the door to the clerk's office began to turn.

"Tomorrow, then," Pete insisted. "Eight o'clock at night. See ya then." And he disappeared out the door into the hall just as the clerk's door swung open and Marti stormed in past a protesting Sam.

"And I'm telling *you*," she barked at him, "this can't wait. If I'd wanted to see him tomorrow, I'd have come tomorrow."

Sam gave Andrew a half-indignant, half-pleading look. Andrew shrugged and nodded. He'd better listen to her. Sam withdrew, presumably to chew on a few tenpenny nails.

"Sister Locatelli—" Andrew began.

"Marti, for the love of Mike!" she growled. "And if you talk about Pete, make it *Loco*-telli. The man's completely nuts."

"What's the trouble?"

She took a good half-hour to lay it out. It seemed that Pete was not responding well to the increase in love she had been displaying. He cringed visibly at her terms of endearment. A consummate indoorsman, he had suddenly taken to spending a good deal of time outside in some hidden location that she and her cousins could not ascertain. He carried concealed cigarettes in a cooler whenever they traveled away from Gina's house and, while the others went sightseeing, slipped off to indulge in them privately in embarrassingly frequent tobacco orgies. "And to top it off," she snarled, "he's been baiting the kids by asking how they like it here. They love it, but he keeps on talking like Utah's some howling wilderness without a redeeming feature and Chicago's been the center of civilization ever since Rome fell. Like *he's* any authority! If he insists on having a lousy time, that's no reason for him to make sure that we have one too."

Despite Andrew's efforts to soothe her ruffled feelings, Marti raged on seemingly interminably. At length, by quoting every scripture he could recall about marital happiness and the power of love—except, of course, those written by the Apostle Paul—he mollified her enough to consent to give the trial more time. "The Pete you married is worth a week more, isn't he?" he entreated.

"Yes, curse him," she muttered ominously.

By the time Andrew was able to usher her out the door, the hour was ten minutes past eight. He sprinted home to find Jeanette sitting aimlessly in the living room beside their temple bags, staring at her hands, while the stereo system played Haydn's "Clock" Symphony in the background. His apologies sounded flimsy, even to himself, and her attempts to be cheerfully gracious about it seemed flat and forced. A hectic drive got them to the temple in time for the day's last endowment session, but it was a foregone conclusion that Neville's would be closed and the park lane veiled in blackness long before it ended. The session calmed Andrew's frayed nerves and seemed to put Jeanette in a more naturally tranquil mood, but slurping soft ice cream cones in a booth at an all-night convenience store afterward was a far cry from the intimate, romantic atmosphere he had planned for their time together.

Jeanette had fielded three phone calls for him that evening, none of which boded well for more time with her tomorrow. One was from Andrew's supervisor at the base, begging him to come in tomorrow morning for "just an hour or two"—military code for at least half a day—of overtime help in preparing a critical report. Another was from Todd Mikesell, who had undertaken to schedule nine more interviews for him tomorrow afternoon. ("The last nine! We'll have it all done in one week!" he had exclaimed proudly, leaving Andrew to wonder what world record he was hoping to break by doing so.) And the third was from Del Jarvis, explaining that he and Irene would be available between six and eight in the evening to translate for Andrew's interview with the Slovenian family if that would be convenient. This was the first time Andrew had considered the immigrants' situation.

"I guess I'm the nearest they have to a bishop, aren't I?" he mused gloomily.

"I think so, since atheists don't usually have bishops to look out for them," Jeanette replied tactfully. "It's the right thing to do."

"I was really hoping to make up to you for this evening," he demurred gently, putting an arm around her waist.

"Oh, you will," she said, kissing him lightly on the jaw. "I'll see to it. How about after eight tomorrow?"

"That would be—" he began eagerly, then he stopped abruptly as he remembered Pete. "Great, except for one thing," he finished unhappily. "Another interview."

"Then we'll make it after that," Jeanette amended. "I'll bet I can outwait any interviewee in the ward."

"I hope so," Andrew said. *I* really *hope so,* he added to himself. Aloud, he asked, "What cheer on the family history front?"

Jeanette hesitated. "Not much to report so far," she answered in an uncharacteristically evasive manner. She didn't meet his eyes as she said it.

"You will keep trying, though, won't you?" he pressed anxiously.

This time she did look at him. "Yes," she affirmed softly. "I will."

* * *

Jeanette sent Andrew off to work with some of her best banana-nut waffles under his belt and the promise of a hearty lunch before his interviews began at two. After washing the dishes, cleaning an already clean house, disposing of the week's laundry in two loads, and setting a pot of meaty homemade soup to simmer, she found herself at loose ends. Fighting her disinclination, she retrieved the folders containing Irene's family history lines and worked through them again, printing out the missing family group sheet, meticulously sorting the records, and entering the data from each into the computer file that Andrew had begun on Monday—could it have been just six days ago? The entire world had turned upside down since then.

She was combing through the records yet again and adding seemingly insignificant bits of information to the computer file when Andrew arrived home with mere minutes to spare before his afternoon interviews began. He gulped the soup appreciatively, grabbed some bread and butter for the road, kissed her hastily, and was gone. She watched wistfully from the window as he strode toward the meetinghouse. *This breakneck schedule can't continue much longer,* she thought. *Either Andrew will wear out, or I'll find a way to sabotage it.*

Awakening her slumbering computer, she examined the partial pedigree she had created for Susan. For reasons she could not fully explain, she had entered the entire line between Susan and Thomas and Mary Barnes, even though it made no sense to look for errors any further back than the generation of Susan's mother, Linda. In that generation, she had to admit, there was plenty of room for either errors or family skeletons.

Closing her eyes, she envisioned the pedigree line as she always did—in vignettes. Thomas and Mary Barnes and their only surviving child, fourteen-year-old John, had been baptized into The Church of Jesus Christ of Latter-day Saints somewhere in England in 1864. They had emigrated from there to Utah by steamship, rail, and wagon two years later. She pictured the little family, clothed in patched garments stained from weeks of travel, within a rickety railroad coach, creeping across Nebraska at the amazing speed of twenty miles an hour toward the western trail-head, where wagons and ox teams from Utah Territory waited to carry them on the final leg of their long journey.

Mary had survived less than a decade on the harsh Utah frontier, but it had been long enough to see her son marry Annie Rogers, another English convert, in the Endowment House and to hold her first grandchild, a boy named Joseph Lehi Barnes. Jeanette imagined the baby, only a few days old, clothed in a lacy, beribboned dress and tiny cap, snuggled in the arms of his adoring grandmother as she lay dying in Centerville, Utah, on a mattress stuffed with corn shucks.

Joseph had grown strong and devout in the faith, serving a mission to the Native Americans in southern Utah before marrying Rose Davis in 1898. Jeanette pictured Rose, clothed in a high-necked white shirtwaist with long, full sleeves and a dark, well-fitting, bell-shaped cashmere skirt, eagerly leaning out the window as her husband-to-be, his hair parted neatly in the middle, jauntily drove his buggy into her parents' yard in Farmington on their wedding morning.

Five years later, their third child and first daughter received during her infant blessing the elegant and fashionable name of Bertha Lillian. Jeanette imagined the proud father, his thick fringe of mustache concealing the smile on his lips as he bore the little infant in his arms to the front of the chapel and there held her aloft for the admiration of his fellow Saints.

From there, the story grew sadder. Fifteen-year-old Bertha and three of her brothers and sisters became orphans in 1918, when the Spanish influenza swept their parents and the rest of their siblings away in its wave of death. Coping as best she could, Bertha had enrolled in a commercial college, become skilled at stenography and typewriting, cut her hair in a short bob, and entered the business world as a career office worker. Her demure beauty had caught the eye of Lyle Rodney Newman, a young coworker, somewhat worldly but with a distinguished pioneer heritage and a promising future. When, after several years of determined courtship, he promised her a temple marriage, she had accepted him. Jeanette imagined what a lovely pair they might have made in their 1924 wedding portrait: he in a black, three-piece suit with gold watch chain, and she in her long, classically draping white silk gown and a floor-length veil tumbling from the back of her beaded headband.

Life had gone well for some time, although Jeanette gathered from Russ Newman's retelling of the story that Lyle's commitment to the gospel had varied as often and extremely as did the weather, to the great disappointment of his wife. Nevertheless, she had conscientiously led him and their seven children through fifteen years of active Church participation. A serious illness contracted in 1939, while she served as a busy Relief Society president ministering to several young widows, had led to her untimely death. And that had led to chaos within the family that so depended upon her. Lyle, who held the

Church responsible for his tragic loss, never entered a meetinghouse again. For the remainder of his life—another forty-seven years—he had bitterly denounced the religion and the God that had deprived him of the woman he loved. And his four youngest sons, all under the age of eight when their mother died, had followed his lead.

Russ himself was the son of one of these lost lambs. His conversion and baptism had come late in his teens amid the opposition of most of his family. It had been Susan who had sent the missionaries to him. Susan, daughter of Linda Jewel, the third child of Lyle and Lillian, had grown up in a family free of the anti-Mormon rancor Russ had known. Nevertheless, Linda and her elder siblings, Cleve and Phyllis, had known their share of grief and doubt following their mother's death. Cleve had taken refuge in the Church, depending on his priesthood leaders to give him the faithful guidance that his father would not. Lyle, in his anger, had threatened and, Russ had hinted, even beaten Cleve for his refusal to give up his Church activity. At age sixteen, two years following his mother's death, Cleve had broken with the family and gone to live in the household of the bishop.

Jeanette shuddered as she considered the magnitude of that action. If Lyle had been angry at the Church and its leaders before, he must have been furious after Cleve left. That one action had effectively ended the possibility that Lyle would ever return to the faith of his fathers. But, she admitted, there was every indication that no matter what his children did, Lyle would not have returned. Perhaps Cleve had hoped to jolt his father into reconsidering his position; perhaps he had simply weighed the value of his testimony against the price of living with his spiritually deficient father and had made the best decision he could. Either way, the result had been that Cleve, at least, had remained faithful.

Cleve's departure had left Phyllis and Linda in a difficult situation. Younger and more dependent on their father, traumatized by their mother's death and their father's rage against Cleve and the church in which they had been baptized, they had coped in different ways. Phyllis, naturally extroverted, had taken a permanent seat on a social merry-go-round overlapping both worlds. Boldly exploiting her father's partiality toward her, she had flitted from church party to public dance hall, from MIA classmates to school chums of questionable repute, never giving him a chance to guess where she really stood. As a result, Russ claimed, she had confused herself as well. It was the common opinion of the extended family that her death in Salt Lake City at the age of twenty-one was the result of heavy alcohol consumption at a sorority party.

Linda, according to Russ, had retreated into a deep, long-term solitude of depression. She had attended church on Sundays with Phyllis but had spurned all weekday activities sponsored by church or school. Politely but firmly, she had rebuffed even direct, personal invitations from well-meaning Church members who had known and loved her for years. No one using any amount of persuasion could coax from her any statement of her feelings for or against the Church. "No one knew where she stood until she came back from that year with Cleve," Russ had told Jeanette. "But the guy she was going with before she left—he was bad news. My uncles said so, and they were pretty bad news themselves, so they would have known."

Jeanette hadn't wanted to pry at the time, but perhaps the time had come to ask Russ what kind of "bad news" that former boyfriend had been. Bad enough to compromise a girl's honor and then break up with her? Had Linda wanted to escape from more than just memories when she moved to Parowan? She envisioned a young woman of twenty-one, pertly coiffed with short bangs and tight pageboy curls, clad in a full-skirted dress of midcalf length, trying to find her place in the unsettled world following the Second World War without the benefit of a mother's counsel and well aware of her father's strong prejudices.

Whether or not she had something to hide, what would be more natural than to flee to the home of the one relative who had stayed strong through it all?

So she was back where she had begun. Shaking her head in frustration, Jeanette closed the manila folders and put her computer back to sleep. It was time to prepare dinner.

Andrew made another flying visit for dinner, wolfing down a pork chop, baked potato, and salad in record time before returning to the meetinghouse for his appointment with the Slovenians and the Jarvises. A little pettishly, Jeanette reflected that if she'd wanted to be lonely, she could just as well have remained single. *It isn't Andrew's fault,* she lectured herself. *And it won't be like this forever.* But it didn't help that the symphony orchestra on their favorite classical radio station was performing Strauss's "Perpetual Motion" in the background.

Shutting off the music, she made a phone call to Russ Newman. Linda's former boyfriend, he told her, was exactly the kind of bad news that she had feared. "He was slick and persuasive, and he didn't have a scruple in his whole character—a one-man baby boom, to put it bluntly. And he stayed that way until his dying day. As for how far he got with Aunt Linda, I don't know anything for sure. None of us ever asked her. But it's a possibility."

Weary and discouraged, Jeanette put the folders away and scanned the shelves for a book that could take her mind off this whole situation. *Wuthering Heights?* No way—a dose of Heathcliff would be all she needed to sour her on men forever. *The Vicar of Wakefield?* Not likely—too many lovely women stooping to folly. *Mansfield Park?* Absolutely not—the conniving Crawfords and the gullible Bertrams were the last people she wanted to endure at this point. *The Scarlet Letter?* Good heavens, no! Finally she settled on *A Tale of Two Cities.* Murder, revolt, treason, *la guillotine,* and implacable revenge might not make for relaxing reading, but at least they provided an escape from the present reality.

* * *

As Andrew entered the convenience store at eight thirty-five and scanned the tables in the deli area, his first hope was that Pete had either changed his mind or given up and gone home to Gina's. Two and a half hours of wading through policies and protocol in English and Slovenian to provide for the refugees had worn him to a frazzle. But no—Pete sat slumped in the corner booth, with the infamous collapsible cooler on the table in front of him.

Gathering his remaining energy, Andrew crossed the room and slid in opposite him. "I've looked over your résumé," he began, pushing the printed sheet across the table. "It's . . . a start, but . . . I think you may be too clear on what kind of organization you were working for." He read aloud, "'Researcher/analyst: Tracked street gangs and assessed their activities for competing interests.' That word *competing* may be a little too revealing for your purposes."

Pete shook his head miserably. "I worked that sentence over for three hours. That was the best I could do, ya know? You should've seen it when I started."

Andrew sighed, wishing that he had Jeanette's gift with words. "Let's leave it for now, and I'll do some thinking. But now we need to find a way to beef up those credentials."

Pete gazed blearily at him. "Hey, bishop, we can't beef up what isn't there to beef, ya know? I started work with the business when I was still in high school. I've never worked for anyone else. The boys'll give me good references, sure, but who's going to listen to *them*?" He held out the crumpled piece of paper containing the website addresses that Andrew had compiled. "All these places want you to fill out an application, all of 'em want prior job experience, and all of 'em want the truth. If I tell it, either they won't believe me or they'll call the cops."

Andrew couldn't deny the difficulties. He sent a fleeting prayer for inspiration heavenward, but he could almost hear it bump against the ceiling and stick there. "Well, hang on to the list. We'll think of something. The Lord doesn't give us commandments we can't keep," he said, almost at random. "Let's pray and sleep on it tonight, and maybe something will occur to us tomorrow."

"I've been doin' that for years," Pete murmured, shoving the wadded list of Internet sites into his pocket and grasping his cooler.

Andrew eyed it with suspicion. "How's it going with quitting smoking?"

Pete groaned. "I don't even want to think about it." He slid out from behind the table and stood up. "Gotta go. I need to stop at the grocery store and pick up some celery for Gina." He gagged slightly on the word *celery*.

Andrew stood too. "You don't care for celery, I take it."

"I hate the stuff. It's poison with strings running through it. Hey, what's up?" Pete asked, suddenly noticing the flashing of white and colored lights at the edge of the service station's parking area.

Andrew looked out the window. "That's got to be Chief Ridley. He's looking at something on the wall of the freeway overpass."

Pete looked alert for the first time. "It's happening right by my car. Let's check it out," he said, leading the way to the door.

"Hang on," Andrew protested. "You're walking straight into the arms of the police!"

"Hey, they don't know who I am. Here in Utah, I'm just another tourist, ya know? Besides, I gotta get to my car sometime."

A patrolman had aimed a flashlight on the concrete wall so that it illuminated three bizarre, spray-painted symbols. Chief Ridley was examining them closely, cursing freely. "Get away with this in my town? I don't think so."

"What's going on, chief?" Pete asked coolly, stopping beside him.

"Gangs. They've finally made it here. Insolent punks! Now I've got to root them out. And I don't know beans about that whole scene. I've been in small towns for too long. Looks like three of them, and I haven't got a clue who they are."

Pete squinted up at the graffiti and chuckled. "Naw, probably just two and some wannabes. And none of them's got anything like experience. Those look like kindergarten scrawls." He pointed. "The red one on the right is the Narkosos. They're based in Phoenix. Mostly Latino membership. The uniform is low-hanging knee shorts and black T-shirts, and they go in big for tattoos. Red's their fight color, so they're sending out a challenge." He pointed again, this time at the middle symbol. "That blue one's the Boomers, out of L.A. They're Polynesians, mostly. They're harder to pick out, 'cause they wear flowered shirts buttoned over their tees and look pretty normal most of the time. Scarcely any tattoos. But when they're gettin' ready to fight, they unbutton the shirts. And that one on the left," he said, chuckling again, "is a real clumsy forgery of the KWK symbol. I can show you the Internet site they copied it from. See, they put that bar across the middle as if it's part of the symbol. It's actually part of another symbol that was underneath in that photo. Just happened to be the same color."

Andrew stared at Pete, completely stunned. *Why doesn't he just ask for the handcuffs and put them on himself while he's at it?* he wondered.

Chief Ridley, on the other hand, was regarding Pete with awe that approached the level of hero worship. "You're really up on this stuff," he said finally. "What else can you tell me?"

Pete shrugged. "Just that the Narks and the Boomers will probably be staging a fight somewhere near here soon. Have you got officers posted at the schools?"

"There's the DARE officers at the high school and the junior high."

Andrew noticed Pete's puzzled look. "DARE's a drug-use prevention program," he explained.

Pete nodded. "Well, have 'em watch for Latinos with their shorts nearly hangin' off, ya know? The day they come wearing red and purple T-shirts is the day they'll fight. And have 'em keep an eye out for Polynesians with unbuttoned shirts, too. If they get a chance to listen in and hear where the meetin' place is, you can have patrolmen there to break it up and maybe arrest the leaders."

Chief Ridley gave a long, low whistle of approval. "You're good, you know that? How long are you in town for?"

Pete shrugged again. "Another week for sure—maybe longer."

"You want some work?" asked the chief, rubbing his hands together briskly. "Bet I could find you some. You got a résumé or something?"

Pete nervously twitched the unfolded paper in his hand and glanced fearfully at Andrew, who winced and shook his head slightly. But the chief had already seen it. Seizing it out of Pete's hand, he said, "I'll be in touch. You're staying at Roylances', around the block from my girl Tif, right?"

Pete looked as though knowing where or who Tif might be was the least of his worries at the moment.

"Right," Andrew concurred uneasily. Then he added, "Haven't you got some celery to pick up, Brother—?" He choked off before using the name.

Pete gagged slightly and glanced at his watch. "Holy cow! I've gotta scramble. If I break curfew, Gina'll have my hide. So long," he added over his shoulder as he climbed into his car.

"How are your girls doing, chief?" Andrew asked by way of a quick diversion.

"Fine, so they tell me. I'll be seeing 'em in church tomorrow. They all said they're coming, and I'll be there to help tend Tif's kids. This grandparent thing's a lot of work, but it sure can be fun."

"This afternoon I worked with your Slovenian guests to find a place to live. There's a vacant apartment a block or two away. The landlord's a member of our ward, and he's willing to negotiate on the rent. We can fill the cupboards for them. And if you need to replenish your own food supply, let me know tomorrow, and we'll get a food order going."

Chief Ridley smiled broadly. "That's what I like about you folks. You take care of each other. It'd make my day if one of you ever got to be president."

Andrew would have laughed if he could have found the energy. As it was, he managed a very weak smile.

"But, listen, Mr. McCammon," the chief added, stepping closer and lowering his voice slightly. "With all due respect, leavin' your brand-new wife for all these hours isn't goin' to make your family life any better. Take a tip from an old family man and get yourself home. Maybe pick up a box of chocolates on the way. Help her remember why she married you."

Andrew gritted his teeth. *You could slice the irony with a knife,* he thought grimly. "Thanks for the tip, chief. I believe I'll do that."

The convenience store had hefty, trucker-sized chunks of fudge but no chocolates. The all-night supermarket had a pathetic, picked-over selection of boxed chocolates left from Mother's Day. Bolstering his selection with a midsummer nosegay, he headed home, stifling yawns and wondering if Jeanette had even bothered to wait up for him.

There was no scented candlelight or soft music tonight. She was sitting up in bed, her reading lamp on full, deeply engrossed in a thick tome by Charles Dickens. She jumped visibly when he entered the room but warmed up delightedly at the sight of the chocolates and flowers. Playfully, she split a couple of chocolates with him, then she left the room to find a vase for the flowers. Andrew lay down to rest for just a moment as he waited for her to return.

The next thing he heard was the sound of his alarm going off. It was six in the morning, and sunlight was filtering through the blinds. He was still lying on top of the bed in his suit pants and crumpled white shirt. Leadership meetings would start in half an hour.

He turned his head to look at Jeanette. She was sleeping quietly, but her lips formed a pitiful little pout, and there were traces of what might have been dried tears on her cheeks.

CHAPTER 9
Day of Rest

As if to compensate for the marathon week, Andrew's first block of Sunday meetings went beautifully. The morning's leadership meetings ran as smoothly as a freshly oiled motor. Steve Roylance conducted sacrament meeting with the utmost dignity, and nearly all the ward members receiving new callings were present to be sustained. All Andrew needed to do, once he had overseen the blessing and passing of the sacrament, was to listen to the discourses and observe his ward members.

Having been forewarned, he was not surprised to see Chief Ridley and his wife in the congregation, entertaining two restless grandchildren. Next to them, enthroned in the middle of the back row, sat Tiffany, freshly sustained as Primary secretary, with Rhett sitting protectively by her side and adjusting a pair of small footstools for her whenever she needed to shift her heavily casted legs. On the other side of them were the elder Barlows, looking slightly ill at ease, as if they expected someone to demand at any moment what they thought they were doing there. They could not have chosen a better Sunday to return, Andrew reflected, since very few in the ward would realize that they were not regular attendees.

He was more surprised to see, on the far left side of the back row, the Slovenian family, with the Jarvises seated on either side of them, busily translating in a pair of steady whispers. Between the immigrant children sat a girl whom Andrew tentatively identified, on the basis of family resemblance, as Chief Ridley's youngest daughter.

Close to the front sat Jeanette, fresh and lovely in a tailored suit of pale green, at one end of a long row that otherwise contained exclusively Roylances, Modonis, and Locatellis. Pete, at the far end from Jeanette, spent a good deal of the time fidgeting nervously. Marti, sitting next to him, looked as if she wanted nothing more than to give him a swift jab to the ribs with her elbow, but she gazed determinedly ahead at the speakers without even a glance his way. Andrew had to concede that her forbearance was remarkable, the more so because Pete left the meeting four times for no apparent reason. He had already been closeted by Pete, in a state of near panic, earlier this morning. Now that Chief Ridley had his résumé, complete with full name, hometown, and thinly veiled prior employment record, Pete was convinced that his arrest was imminent. The fact that the chief was in attendance at sacrament meeting could not possibly have helped Pete's unsettled state of mind.

Scattered among the other congregants were the four middle Ridley girls, alternating each moment of rapt attention with several more moments of whispered, giggly exchanges with their young hostesses. Having met so many of his ward members only once, Andrew spent a good deal of time matching faces with names. But his eyes kept straying back to Jeanette. Hers was easily the most attractive face out there. Had it really been less than two months ago that he had sat near the front of the chapel watching Jeanette, in her teal dress, speak through a migraine headache to exhort the members to do their family history? So much had happened since then! For one thing, he had become the most fortunate man on earth. Loving Jeanette was worth it all—worth any number of ward crises, welfare challenges, and Locatellis.

* * *

There was one advantage, Jeanette mused dryly, to being married to the bishop. It was expected of him to preside over sacrament meeting, which meant that he would have to sit still on the stand for seventy minutes each week. During that time, she would have a guaranteed opportunity to gaze at the man she had married.

She sighed without realizing it. It wasn't that she begrudged the time he was spending in his new calling. After all, she had been certain since before he proposed marriage that he would someday be a bishop. She was not—absolutely refused to be—the kind of wife who demanded the lion's share of her husband's attention. It was just the ever-present, unwelcome suspicion that she wasn't doing enough to sustain him. He seemed so tired. She was certain that Susan would have known exactly what to do to ease the load of stress he bore. What was Jeanette failing to do? How could she help him?

She shook her head to clear it. The tranquility of sacrament meeting would soon end, and instead of absorbing it for later spiritual energy, she was squandering it on self-accusations. She tried to pick up the thread of the speaker's discourse.

But she became entirely distracted once she discerned, to her great pleasure, that Andrew seemed to be paying a good deal of visual attention to her. And each time their eyes met, his mouth lifted slightly in a smile. Tired or not, he *did* look awesomely handsome in his gray suit, with those matching touches of gray at his temples. *Flirting from a distance isn't*—Jeanette paused and twitched her shoulders uncomfortably—*isn't the best reason for coming to sacrament meeting,* she finished lamely. *Oh, Father, it isn't terribly sinful of me, is it?*

She felt a certain warmth. It didn't exactly communicate reassurance, but she sensed patient understanding. Sighing, she tried again to focus on the speaker at the pulpit.

As the meeting ended and Jeanette arose to go and prepare her classroom, she stole a last glance at Andrew. Blowing her a kiss was, she recognized, out of the question, but he did flout the decorum of the stand so far as to wink at her. She smiled back, blushing slightly. Then, filled with a pleasant, tingly sensation, she proceeded to class.

There was little chance to spare thereafter to think about anything else. Beginning a new class was usually an exercise in dealing with chaos, but on this day, the presence of the Modonis and Locatellis added to the confusion. While the other three fired questions at her, Pete kept leaving and returning at what seemed like five-minute intervals. *Nicotine addiction must be terrible,* she thought as she watched him bolt out the classroom door yet again following the closing prayer.

Gina had everything well in hand for Relief Society. Except for a general introduction session in which each sister stood and stated her name, followed by the distribution of a newly prepared ward list and envelopes containing visiting teaching assignments, it would have seemed no different from the last Relief Society meeting she had conducted two weeks previously. The lesson, beautifully presented by Gina's new education counselor, set a high standard for those to follow in coming weeks.

Andrew had warned Jeanette at bedtime the night before that he would be late to dinner due to the massive numbers of ward members to be set apart in their new callings. She was, therefore, beginning the walk home alone when a familiar voice hailed her.

"Mrs. McCammon?"

It was Chief Ridley.

"I'm tryin' to write a couple of reports," he called, gradually lowering his voice as he closed the distance between them, "and I've got some word hang-ups. Would you say that callin' the Slovenian fellow 'an unsuspicious death under suspicious circumstances' is accurate? My wife, Annabelle, says it's confusing."

Jeanette considered. "You might try 'death from natural causes followed by burial under suspicious circumstances,'" she ventured.

"Yeah, that'll work. Now, can you tell me what's the formal name for a person who knows about street gangs? There's some academic term that's escaping me. Antag . . . no, antar . . . darn, I can't get it."

"Did you say *street gangs*?"

"Yeah, someone who knows how they dress, what their habits and high-signs are, what kind of leadership structure they've got, how they relate to each other . . ."

Jeanette frowned in concentration. "A sociologist? Maybe a psychologist?"

"Naw, I'm sure it starts with an A. Something like antharific . . ."

"Maybe an anthropologist? An urban anthropologist?"

"That's it! This guy didn't even know what to call himself. Looked as phony as all-get-out. Oh, and by the way," he continued, "you and your hubby are invited to Tif's tonight at eight for a family home whatever-it-is. We'll all be there. Rhett works swing tomorrow, see, so it's gotta be tonight. Tif especially wanted you and the bishop to come."

Jeanette swallowed her disappointment at the loss of another restful evening with Andrew. "We'd be honored. May I supply some refreshments?"

"If you like," he answered indifferently. "Annabelle and Donna Barlow prob'ly have that covered, but more never hurts. Oh, and Tif would like your husband to give a lesson on growing in the gospel, whatever that means."

Jeanette swallowed again. "Uh . . . we'll see what we can do."

"He'll do a great job. That's one good man you got there. Clean as a whistle. Even if he does meet folks with gangland connections late at night in odd places, he's bound to have a good reason. Well, they're waitin' for me."

He left Jeanette totally bewildered.

She arrived home to find several frantic messages from Fiona on the answering machine. "Dad, Nan, I'm *really* worried about Mark. He was supposed to meet us for church, and he didn't come. He won't answer his home phone, and he's turned his cell phone off. Please, call just as soon as you can." The succeeding messages repeated the same themes in more desperate tones. Jeanette dialed Fiona's cell number with shaking fingers.

"Did you find him?" she blurted in response to Fiona's greeting.

"Yes." Fiona's voice was gravelly with exasperation. "We went over to his apartment and pounded on the door for half an hour before we got hold of the landlord and borrowed a key. Mark was huddled under the bedcovers the whole time, moping. I gave him the scolding of his life—at least I tried, but it's hard to scold someone when you're hugging him and crying your eyes out at the same time."

"He's safe, then?"

"For now—unless I change my mind and decide to kill him after all."

"Fiona," chided Jeanette, smiling in spite of herself, "this isn't like you."

"I'm sorry, Nan, but I'm at my wit's end. I've tried every technique I've ever heard of or read about, and nothing does any good." Her voice began to tremble with righteous indignation. "And he shouldn't be doing this to a pregnant woman."

"You're right," Jeanette agreed. "It may be time to call in the big guns."

There was silence on Fiona's end for a moment. "What do you have in mind?"

"The twins."

Fiona drew an ecstatic breath. "Of course! They'll browbeat him in stereo—and they'll *never* give up. I'll call them right now."

As she waited for a return call from Fiona or the welcome sound of Andrew opening the front door, Jeanette prepared dinner and whiled away the time by reading dessert recipes and comparing them to the ingredients in the kitchen cupboards. She had just decided on triple-chocolate brownies—the more endorphin release, the better—when Fiona called back. "Eric and Kevin are both taking tomorrow off, and they've already phoned Mark's supervisor and scheduled tomorrow off for him too. *And* they've got onto the Internet and booked three tickets on that steam train ride east of the mountains. They'll dress him and carry him to the car bodily if they have to."

"Pure genius," breathed Jeanette. She knew that Mark had loved steam trains from the time he was a small boy. She also knew the train's location and general schedule. An hour's drive each way and nearly four hours on the train would have Mark surrounded with twins for most of the day. He wouldn't stand a chance of getting away from them. "They know what to say, don't they?"

"I've coached them. Nothing negative about Alyssa or her parents, nothing about any prettier or nicer girls out there somewhere. Just plenty of assurance that this is all part of God's plan for them and that everything will work out for the best. And they've got to spend some time listening too."

"It sounds like a winning strategy."

"Please tell Dad. We need to pray for them all."

"I will."

She told Andrew over dinner about Mark's emotional lapse and the projected train ride, but she made no mention of Irene's letter or her own dwindling hopes. Andrew seemed troubled enough as it was. The news that they were expected at the Barlows' for home evening and that he was to give the lesson didn't help his mood. "Oh, man! Besides being a bishop, now I'm a circuit preacher too! Let's hope nobody else gets any ideas."

To encourage him, she cut the brownies and gave him a generous portion in advance. He ate it while thumbing through his scriptures and scribbling notes, stopping only long enough to remark, "This brownie is terrific," and "I'd better have a glass of milk with this, or I'll be bouncing off the ceiling."

As it turned out, his hasty preparations were more than adequate. He got about five minutes' worth of basic doctrine in before Tiffany took over and mapped out individual and family perfection schedules for her husband, children, parents, sisters, and in-laws. Her total confidence commanded meek obedience from all; Jeanette had to hide a smile when even Chief Ridley responded, "Yes, ma'am," without a hint of sarcasm. Before the refreshments were served, the elder Barlows had committed to attend temple preparation classes along with their son and daughter-in-law, the entire Ridley family had agreed to hear at least two lessons from the full-time missionaries and to read ten pages from the Book of Mormon in family study, and the chief had sworn off swearing.

Jeanette had planned to bow out of the evening as soon as possible, but Tiffany had other plans. Cornering Andrew near the refreshment table, she committed him to set up a temple preparation class and call a teacher within the next month. Then she buttonholed Jeanette and pleaded for the triple-chocolate brownie recipe. When they left the Barlows' little home, it was nine thirty, and the gathering was still in high gear.

* * *

Andrew walked slowly on the way home, relishing the feel of the evening breeze in his hair and Jeanette's hand in his. This was a magical moment, with no cell phones, no pending interviews, and no one near but the woman he cherished. Releasing her hand, he slipped his arm around her waist. She leaned her silvery head against his shoulder, and for a moment, life could not have seemed more heavenly or complete. They were companionably silent until they drew even with the walkway leading to the Roylances' front porch.

"Do you know," he whispered into her ear, "that I nearly kissed you for the first time right here? The only thing that stopped me was Gina coming to the door."

It was exactly the wrong thing to say. Instantly, the door flew open and Gina emerged.

"Just the two we wanted to see. Where have you been? We've been phoning all evening." She stalked down the walkway, and three became an immediate crowd. "We want you both to come to family home evening tomorrow. Jeanette, how about bringing some of your fresh apple cookies? The kids love those. And Andrew, you can give us the lesson. Something on living the gospel better would be just the thing. How does six thirty sound? That'll give us plenty of time before curfew."

So much for the mood, thought Andrew. "Well, I . . . I think we . . ." He looked helplessly at Jeanette.

"We just happen to have the very lesson you want," Jeanette said a little too brightly. "We'll be there."

"Good. Vinnie and Cat haven't been having good luck with their home evenings, so they want to see how it works. Pete hasn't got a clue, of course. See you then." With a wave so brief that it was more of a salute, she retreated inside and shut the door.

Andrew scowled in the darkness. Jeanette took his arm gently. "Sorry, dear," she said in a more genuine tone. "But Gina checks in with Tiffany Barlow every day, and Tiffany tells all. In fact, she might have given Gina the idea. If we turn down the Roylances' invitation after accepting the Barlows', things could get really sticky."

Andrew sighed heavily. "I suppose you're right."

"Besides," Jeanette added more lightly as they began to walk again, "you make such a cute circuit preacher."

"Just for that . . ." retorted Andrew, drawing her into the shadow of a convenient tree.

It was a long and blissful kiss.

CHAPTER 10
Friends, Foes, Failures

Monday morning dawned in an appropriate degree of overcast gloom. After Andrew had breakfasted and departed for work, Jeanette mulled over the disappointing end of their Sunday evening together. Upon arriving home, Andrew had found no fewer than eleven telephone messages awaiting him. Other than the five from Gina, all concerned arrangements to help the Slovenian family move into their new home the next day. All required several urgent phone calls each to settle the questions raised. It was eleven o'clock by the time the last phone call was concluded. As Andrew had prepared for bed, he had outlined for her the seven new items on his to-do list for tomorrow, four of which would need to be completed before he left for work.

"But couldn't your financial clerk take care of those?" Jeanette had asked anxiously.

"Normally, yes," Andrew had wearily explained. "But he left town this afternoon for a week. Sam Taylor could handle them too, but he's gone for the next two days."

"Could I do them? You have so much to do already."

"Not possible, dear, but thanks for the thought."

She had bit her lip, volunteered to voice their couple prayer, and then crawled sadly into bed. Discussion of Irene's letter would have to wait another day or two.

Now, in what light of day there was, she asked herself what Susan would do. Susan would know how to be the unquestioningly patient, loving, and supportive wife a bishop ought to have. She would find some practical way to ease her husband's burdens and to comfort her bereaved son. But what? Clean an already clean house yet again? Continue the increasingly futile pursuit of Irene Jarvis's birth lineage? Bake ten dozen apple cookies for this evening? There *had* to be something more useful than any of those options.

At length, she grabbed her car keys and headed out the door. The Slovenian refugees were moving into their new apartment today, and she might as well help them. They owned so little that there wouldn't be much to do, but it was better than doing nothing.

It turned out to be time well spent. Gina welcomed her gratefully; she was evidently nervous about leaving her company to fend for themselves for very long. Once Del Jarvis arrived, a single trip in two cars was enough to transport the entire family, their escorts, and all their worldly possessions from the Ridleys' house to their new lodgings a mere two blocks away. Then, while Gina and Del went with Lenka to the bishops' storehouse to fill a food order, Jeanette helped the children and their grandmother to arrange their few possessions in the sparsely furnished little apartment. The tiny, wrinkled woman was amazingly spry and sturdy, and she had a keen sense of humor that transcended the barriers of language and loss to keep Jeanette and the children giggling.

With everything neatly disposed, the four of them were relaxing in the living room when the doorbell rang. Tadej went to answer it and electrified them all with a cry of joy. "Vladi!"

They rushed to the door to find him embracing a large, chocolate-colored Labrador-mix dog who was licking his face eagerly. Holding the animal's leash was a bemused, middle-aged man who introduced himself as the landlord. "Seems you already know my friend here," he commented.

"He is our dog before we move away," Tadej explained.

"All this time I thought I had a way with dogs," the landlord remarked dryly. "I whistled to him and called him 'Laddie,' and he came right up to me. Now I know why."

Vladi was now warmly and wetly greeting Tadej's sister, little Vesna, who hugged him with equal enthusiasm. Being a gentleman to the core, the landlord immediately offered to return Vladi to the family. But Tadej, regretfully but firmly, refused. "We are poor, cannot feed him. You keep Vladi. Take care of him."

"That I will," the landlord promised. "And you can come to visit him. Is everything going well?"

"Just fine, I think," Jeanette answered on behalf of the family. "The electricity and water are working."

"The gas will be on soon, I hope. I had some concerns about the hookup when the last tenant was moving out, and I've asked a technician to come by and take a carbon monoxide reading. I'm supposed to meet him here."

In less than a minute, the technician arrived. After banishing everyone to the front yard temporarily, he disappeared into the basement. In a few moments, he was back. "The gas is on and burning cleanly. You're all set," he informed the landlord. Patting the dog on the head, he next inquired about the family, whom he recognized from a past service call. "I thought these folks lived a few blocks over from here," he told Jeanette.

"They used to," she concurred. "They've been in Las Vegas since then."

"I remember taking a reading a year or so back at their old house. They were nice folks—brought me a glass of lemonade with ice. Next time I came by, the place was deserted. Well . . . not quite. There was this big dark guy digging in the backyard, but *he* sure didn't seem friendly."

"Digging in the backyard?" Jeanette asked as chills began to come over her.

"Yeah. Some kind of plumbing repair job, I figured, because he had quite a pit opened up. But he wasn't one of the family. At least, the dog didn't act like it. He was growling and snapping at the guy, and the guy was shouting at him and shaking the shovel in his face."

"What was he shouting?"

"Couldn't tell. It wasn't English, I know for sure it wasn't Spanish or Portuguese, and it didn't sound like Italian or French or German either. Sounded like it could have been Russian, or something close to it."

"Uh . . . do you remember when this was, exactly?"

"Mmmm . . . Yeah, in fact. It was the third of April, the day before my wife's birthday."

"And did you get a good look at the man?"

"Better than I wanted. He was ugly to begin with, and he got even uglier when he saw me. I read the meter and got out as fast as I could."

"Could I . . . get your name? I think the police might be interested in that man you saw."

"The police? You figure he was up to something?"

Jeanette hesitated and glanced at the family members behind her. They were still renewing their friendship with Vladi. Only the landlord was listening in closely. "Do you remember reading in the paper about a buried corpse that the police uncovered in a backyard here in town last month?"

Shocked comprehension dawned in both men's faces. "It was at *their* house?" the landlord guessed in a subdued but horrified voice. "Was the dead man someone connected with them?"

"The children's father. He went missing just before they moved. They thought they were going to meet him, but he wasn't at the meeting place."

"Those poor kids!" exclaimed the gas technician. He pulled a pen and a business card from his pocket, circled something on the card, and handed it to Jeanette. "I've marked my cell phone number. Tell the police to call me anytime. If I know anything that could help, I'm more than happy to pass it on."

As soon as he had left, the landlord spoke to Jeanette in a subdued voice. "I suppose the bishop is on top of all this. Please let him know that the family is welcome to stay indefinitely. If he needs to negotiate further on the rent, we can do that."

"Thank you," Jeanette answered quietly, glancing covertly at the children as they gave Vladi a last hug each.

The arrival of Gina, Lenka, and Del with a supply of groceries and household goods was the landlord's cue to depart. In the ensuing confusion, Jeanette took the opportunity to phone Chief Ridley. Though "all tied up"—Jeanette smiled at the image—he was pleased to receive a lead of any kind and promised to send a patrolman immediately to pick up the card and deliver it to the detective assigned to the case.

Groceries were still being shelved when a small police vehicle looking rather like an ultralight truck with a cage in its bed arrived in front of the house. Hurrying out to meet its driver, Jeanette watched a familiar-looking young patrolman emerge from the cab and motion to an excited Irish setter in the cage to sit.

"Your name is . . . Justin. Am I right?" Jeanette inquired tentatively.

"Justin Price at your service, Mrs. McCammon," the young man said. "I'm glad things have gone better for you since you lost your house."

"They have, thanks. And this is Paddy," recalled Jeanette, admiring the setter, who had sniffed out a drug-smuggling operation on one of the most eventful days she had ever lived through.

"Yep. He's my partner, I'm his chauffeur. We call this the Paddy-wagon," he said, pulling a comical face at his own joke.

Jeanette laughed, but remembering the reason for his visit soon sobered her. Retrieving the card from her pocket, she handed it to Justin while explaining briefly what she had learned from the gas technician. Although she was certain that the detective would prefer to get the entire story directly from the eyewitness, it relieved her feelings to tell someone. Justin listened carefully but took no notes.

"Houses typically don't have plumbing connections in the backyard. I would definitely call this suspicious," he assented. "I'll pass this along to the detective right away."

As he was pulling away in the Paddy-wagon, Gina exited the house. "We've stowed everything. Brother Jarvis tells me that the women are ready to start sewing in exchange for the goods. Would you be willing to phone around and see if anyone has a sewing machine to loan them? I've got to get back home."

"I know just the person," Jeanette replied. "Dora Jantzen offered me her machine just before my wedding. She says her eyes are too bad to use it anymore."

"Perfect," Gina concurred with a rare smile. "See you at six thirty."

Sister Jantzen gave willing permission to part with her sewing machine to the Slovenian family, and Del Jarvis offered to transport it and its table to their new home in his truck. Feeling incompetent to explain how it worked to the women, he brought Irene to give them instructions in how to work it. They were adept learners and were plainly delighted with their new skills. Jeanette had remained more out of sociability than anything else, but by the time all this was accomplished, it was midafternoon and time to bake apple cookies and start dinner. Just before leaving, she debated whether to bring up the subject of Irene's parentage again but decided not to. She could not think of anything to ask that Irene might be able to answer, and she didn't want to revive the forced quality that came into the Jarvises' manner whenever the topic arose.

* * *

Andrew arrived home to the mingled odors of spaghetti sauce and baking apple cookies—and the ominous sound of the telephone ringing. Jeanette answered it just as he stepped through the door. "How did it go?" she was asking. "Wait a moment; let me switch over to speaker. Your father just came in, and I'll bet he'll want to hear this too." She touched a button and hung up the receiver.

"We think it went well," came Eric's voice tinnily through the air, along with some faint crackling in the background.

"Even if we do say so ourselves," added Kevin.

"Mark was pretty miserable to start with."

"Yeah, we had to threaten him to get him dressed."

"But once we got into the pickup and on the road, he started to take a little interest."

Andrew knew the twins' tactics. Warily, he asked, "Did he get in voluntarily?"

"Eventually," Kevin answered cheerfully. "We didn't have to use any intimidation."

"No, just gentle shoves at the appropriate moments," Eric clarified.

"Eric drove and I sat by the other door, so he was in between us."

"So he got two earfuls," Andrew surmised.

"All the way there and all the way back," Eric agreed.

"And on the train, too," Kevin put in.

"And we followed Fiona's instructions to the letter."

"The name Jarvis never passed our lips."

"No, we merely gushed about the beauties of nature and the great plan of the Creator."

"Then we invited him to speculate on his part in it."

"And when he started to get negative on the train, Kevin came up with the quote of a lifetime."

"Actually, I got it from general conference several years ago, but it came in handy."

"What was it?" asked Jeanette.

"The one about life being like a ride on an old-fashioned steam train," Eric elaborated. "And how it's slow, smoky, full of flying cinders . . ."

". . . but the trick is to thank the Lord for letting you have the ride," finished Kevin.

Andrew had to admit that the twins had their moments of sheer brilliance. "Wow," he commented. "That would have hit home to Mark. He's been crazy about steam locomotives since before he could talk."

"It seemed to go over well," Kevin admitted.

"He was pretty quiet on the ride home," Eric reported. "But it was a thoughtful quiet, not a depressed one."

"And when we invited him to our place for home evening," Kevin said, "he accepted right away—even knowing that Eric would be here too."

"Hey, Skeezix, how do you know it wasn't *because* I was coming that he said yes?"

Jeanette interrupted apprehensively. "You're sure he didn't say that just to get rid of you? He promised to meet Fiona and Spencer yesterday, but he didn't."

"Not a chance," Eric replied breezily.

"We didn't take him home," Kevin explained. "He's helping Heather and Sheri make the potato salad right now while we grill the hamburgers."

Not for the first time, Andrew reflected that it was a good thing for the world that the twins were on the side of righteousness.

Once the call was ended, Jeanette briefed Andrew on the Slovenian family's move and the gas technician's story as she set the table. The recital was enough to put Andrew's own impending ordeal out of his mind, at least for the moment. "Wow! You *do* have a knack with these things, don't you? Maybe the chief is right."

Jeanette wrinkled her nose in a comic grimace. "Don't encourage him," she begged. "Researching the dead is one thing, but working with dead *bodies* is another."

Following the blessing, Andrew ate with his left hand while putting finishing touches on his home evening lesson with his right hand. "For some reason," he confessed to Jeanette, "it makes me nervous to teach in front of Steve and Gina."

Jeanette chuckled sympathetically. "Steve's a master teacher, but he isn't hard to please. No matter what, he'll smile and thank you and find something to compliment."

"That's true. I guess I'm really more worried about Gina. If she holds me up to Steve's standards, I'm sunk."

"Knowing her, I'm sure she wouldn't have asked you if she hadn't been impressed with your talks when you were on the high council."

Andrew hoped that she was right.

The welcome they received at the Roylance home a few minutes later was unequivocally warm. Of course, the fact that each of them bore a large tray of fresh apple cookies certainly helped. Gina effectively undermined Andrew's shaky confidence by immediately bearing the trays away to the kitchen, threatening the children within an inch of their lives if they swiped so much as a crumb before the end of the lesson, and scolding Pete when he arrived late. "I sent you to buy celery. You didn't have to harvest it."

"Hey, you couldn't pay me enough to harvest those green bundles of warped plywood," he protested grimly, setting two bunches down on the kitchen counter.

"Why two? I asked for one."

"Yeah, well, I got you one on Saturday, and it's gone. I thought I'd save gas by getting a supply now so that you don't send me again tomorrow."

"All right, everyone. Where's the plywoo—celery disappearing to?"

Silence.

Gina glared accusingly around at them. "It isn't that I mind," she snapped, "much. But you could tell me before you clean my supply out. Until further notice, you're all under suspicion. Except Pete," she qualified, glancing at him.

Pete mumbled and retreated to a corner of the living room as Gina commandeered the aid of Jeanette, Cat, and Marti to wash and cut celery for the vegetable tray.

Home evening began five minutes late, presided over and conducted by Steve, whose ever-present smile was not in the least dimmed by Gina's quiet fuming. The business and calendar portion, typically very lively within the Roylance household, was even more so as everyone weighed in with suggestions on how to spend the visitors' last week in Utah—everyone, that was, except the McCammons and Pete. Jeanette, Andrew supposed, either didn't notice Pete's lack of participation or attributed it to willingness to go along with anything. Andrew, however, knew why it didn't matter to Pete, and he began to feel a faint, throbbing ache in his head.

In spite of everything, the lesson went well. The Roylance children led the way with plenty of comments and questions, and Steve, with what little he said, kept drawing the discussion back on topic when it strayed. Pete was unusually attentive. He didn't leave for his usual nicotine breaks. Once the lesson concluded, though, he made a brief stop at the refreshment table and then departed toward his car, carrying a plate containing several cookies and a few fresh vegetables, none of them celery.

The younger Roylance son, Ben, whose assignment was the activity, had selected crab soccer on the front lawn. This proved to be a big hit with his cousins and siblings but effectively relegated the adults to the role of spectators, which most of them seemed not to mind. Pete, when he rejoined the group, seemed a little envious but settled into a lawn chair beside Marti, who greeted him with, "About time . . . sweetheart." Andrew would have laughed aloud at her contrasting tones if he hadn't been so apprehensive about the outcome.

At the height of the game, Andrew sensed a presence behind the line of lawn chairs. He turned in time to see Chief Ridley, in full uniform, tapping on Pete's shoulder. Andrew and Pete bolted to their feet at the same instant.

"Good evening, chief," Andrew said, quickly drawing attention away from the terror-stricken expression on Pete's face.

"Evenin', Mr. McCammon," the chief replied easily. "Could I speak to the two of you privately for a sec?"

Pete seemed to have lost his voice, so Andrew kept talking. "Sure thing," he said in a tone that tried to be casual. "Nice cool breeze we've got, isn't it?" He hoped fervently that the perspiration on his forehead didn't show too much.

"It's been a great day for law enforcement, I can tell you," Chief Ridley replied as he led the two men out of earshot.

Pete gazed desperately at Andrew, who struggled to remain calm.

Turning, the chief smiled benignly. "Well, Mr. Locatelli," he began, "I'd like you to know that you were responsible for today's success. Those two gangs of punks showed up at the high school today with red and purple tees and unbuttoned shirts. The DARE officer listened in and found out the time and place, and we staked it out and stopped the brawl before it even began. We got the local leaders of both groups behind bars right now."

As the chief spoke, Pete relaxed so visibly that Andrew feared he would end up in a heap on the sidewalk.

"Our first gang war is over, and it never even happened, thanks to you. Just thought you might like to know."

Mustering up all his nerve, Pete whispered hoarsely, "No problem."

"I've got some other business with you," the chief continued, causing Pete to go rigid again. "But I've got to get a little more input first. Might take a day or two. So stick around, okay? Now, about the stiff," he said, turning to Andrew.

Pete blanched. Andrew moved slightly farther away from him to ensure that the chief didn't happen to glance back in Pete's direction.

"We found out . . . Y'know, we might want Mrs. McCammon to hear this too," he interrupted himself. "She's the one who gave us the tip we needed."

Uneasily, Andrew beckoned to Jeanette, who had been watching in some puzzlement. She arose and joined them.

"The detective interviewed that gas tech," Chief Ridley told her, "and the subpoenaed phone record arrived the same time. We compared things with the report we got from the widow and her family, and the time frame fits exactly. We figure that whoever buried the guy phoned from here in town and pretended to be him. He told 'em to take the bus to Vegas, see, and then watched the house. As soon as they left, he dug the grave and buried the stiff."

By this time, Pete had realized that this matter concerned no corpses that he knew, and he was nearly reduced to tears of relief. Andrew gently took Jeanette's arm and subtly drew her farther away from Pete. The chief amicably turned with them, so that Pete was nearly behind him.

"He had the dog to contend with, of course, so he didn't dig very deep and didn't stick around to try to make things look less suspicious. Good thing you met up with this gas tech and put two and two together, 'cause none of the neighbors'd noticed anything strange. We thought we had a dead end till today. Now we hafta find the goon and bring him in, but at least we've got a description."

"Is it anyone that the family knows?" asked Jeanette.

"Not too likely. The mom says that they didn't know anyone around here after their sponsor moved. She says until the Jarvises came over, she hadn't heard anyone speak her language since she left Slo-wherever."

"And why would anyone pull a trick like that on them?" she continued.

"Now, there all we can do is guess, but the detective has a theory that whoever it was is in the country illegally and didn't want to get involved with a police investigation—and for sure we'd have investigated anyone who showed up with a dead body. If the evidence was buried in the backyard, see, that'd implicate the family first. Only thing that doesn't make sense is burying him with all his ID still on him. Seems like an illegal alien would take the lot and make use of it."

"Maybe whoever it was just panicked," Andrew offered, casting a warning glance at Pete, who was desperately signaling him from behind the chief's back to cut the conversation short.

"Or maybe he really didn't intend any harm," Jeanette added charitably.

Chief Ridley shook his head tolerantly. "You womenfolk always find a way to put the best face on things. Me, I'm gonna round the jerk up, book him, jail him, and ask questions later. Deep down, most decent people know pretty much by instinct when they're up to somethin' illegal. Don't you think so, Mr. Locatelli?" he asked, turning slightly.

Pete had begun to edge away but froze immediately. "Uh . . . yeah," he managed in a strangled sort of rasp.

"Well, I've kept you all from your fun long enough," the chief said breezily. "Gotta head over to Tif's and read bedtime stories to the grandkids." With a cheery wave, he turned and sauntered off.

Pete sagged as if his backbone had just melted away within him. Jeanette frowned at him in concern. "Are you all right, Pete? You look really worn out."

"Just . . . too much fun all at once, I guess," he muttered. Making a beeline for his empty chair, he snatched up the collapsible cooler from beside it and disappeared into the shadows beside the Roylances' house. Marti watched him leave, shook her head in disgust, and turned back to the game.

Andrew wanted to put some distance between himself and the whole situation. He put his arm around Jeanette and his lips to her ear. "Do you think we can sneak away now? Maybe take a stroll? I've got some compliments that I'm dying to pay you."

Jeanette smiled and brushed his chin with a kiss. "I'll make our excuses." In a few moments, they were admiring a glorious sunset as they strolled home, hand in hand. Andrew still had several compliments left when they came within sight of their front porch, but he stowed them away immediately. Mark was sitting on the steps, waiting for them.

"Hi, Dad, Nan. I just thought I'd stop by and tell you that I think I've made my peace at last."

"Your peace?" Andrew repeated.

"Yes—peace with life, fate, the whole situation. I thought you'd like to know."

"We certainly do want to know," Jeanette said. "Come inside and tell us about it."

Mark's visit stretched to over two hours, but his message was a welcome one. "My mood is still fragile enough that I don't want to run into the Jarvises just yet," he admitted, "but I don't blame them or God anymore. I've still got a purpose on this earth, and I need to find it. And Alyssa—well, you should see her patriarchal blessing. It says that she's got a celestial family waiting for her and a husband who will put her happiness above his own." He paused then went on bravely in a voice only slightly thickened with emotion. "I used to think that would be me, but if it isn't, I'm not going to mess things up for her." He hesitated and then continued. "Even if the guy turns out to be Bill Ross." Mark probably didn't intend the name to come out sounding quite as repellent as it did, Andrew reflected. "She deserves the best man God can give her. I'm just grateful that she ever thought I could be that kind of person."

Andrew's eyes were moist as he embraced his son. "You're on the right track," was all he could say. Jeanette seemed to be more deeply moved even than he was; her eyes streamed tears, and she couldn't choke out more than a few barely comprehensible words.

Once Mark left, Andrew had leisure enough to realize how tired he was. But even more than tired, he felt guilty. Was he the kind of husband who put his wife's happiness above his own? He'd certainly given it scant attention this past week. And with midnight approaching and an early-morning staff meeting looming at work, now seemed far from the ideal time to start.

Jeanette seemed very subdued too, so the two of them, by mutual consent, abbreviated their scripture study to an intensive but brief minimum. As they lay down together after prayer, Andrew drew her close against him. *I'll make it up to her,* he promised himself. *Just as soon as things settle down, I'll give her happiness top priority. I'll make sure that she never regrets marrying me.*

The words had sounded disappointingly hollow even as he thought them. By the time he left for work the next morning, those promises lay shattered all over the kitchen floor.

It was all he could do not to blame Pete for the way things disintegrated. His phone call had awakened Andrew nearly a quarter of an hour before the alarm sounded. "I've gotta meet with you, bishop. Right now."

"For Pete's sake, Brother Locatelli," Andrew said sleepily. "I'm not even out of bed yet."

"All right, I'll wait half an hour. But it's gotta be before you go to work, ya know? This can't wait."

"But I've got—"

"I'll honk when I get there. Be listening, okay? See ya."

Jeanette, bless her sweet heart, had gotten up immediately to fix Andrew a good breakfast. But though he had moved as quickly as he could, he made it to the table in a dead heat with the first honk of Pete's car horn. Jeanette had seemed almost desperate as she said, "Let me put some on a plate and send it with you."

The honking got louder and longer.

"I can't, dear," Andrew had demurred, restlessly looking toward the door. "I need to get out there. He'll wake all the neighbors if he doesn't stop."

"But I want to help," she had protested vigorously. "I can't stand to see you so tired. I want to support you, I want to make your life easier, but nothing I do seems to help."

The honking had become virtually continuous. "Nothing can make a bishop's life easier," he had answered flatly, irritated beyond rationality by the noise. "Not even Susan could—" Horrified, he'd broken off too late. Jeanette's eyes had widened and then slowly shut, tears oozing from under her lashes.

Looking back, he wished that he had dumped his briefcase, grabbed her, and held her tightly to his chest. He wished with all his heart that he had told Pete to leave before he called the SWAT team, then phoned in sick and spent the rest of the morning kissing away her tears. Instead, like an idiot, he had backed toward the door, stammering, "I-I didn't mean that the way it sounded. It's just . . . just that . . . that darned horn of his! Jeanette, I'm so sorry. I only meant—we'll talk this evening, I promise."

But before he had even reached the door, she had turned away.

Now, marching down the walkway toward Pete's car, he could feel the heat radiating from his face, reddened with chagrin and fury. Yanking the door open, he hissed, "Cool it, will you? You'll have the entire police force here any minute! Do you want to land in jail?"

Pete's face, in contrast, was wan. "It don't much matter where they get me. As soon as I've talked to you, I'm turning myself in."

Andrew's anger receded just enough to keep him from retorting, "Good!" Instead, sliding into the passenger seat, he demanded, "What do you mean?"

"I'm goin' to the station and tellin' them to lock me up now. Might as well, ya know? Maybe they'll go easier on me if they don't have to come and get me. It'll be easier on Marti and the kids, too—on everybody—if they don't bash the door down and charge in with guns at the ready."

"Have you been keeping something from me?"

"Nothing, I swear. But you heard the chief. He's got business with me—told me to stick around for a few days. He's gettin' a warrant ready. What else could he mean? And that bit about decent people knowing when they're doin' wrong—it's like he read my mind, ya know?" He sighed. "I dunno why I ever believed it'd be possible to walk away from the business. I shoulda just offered Marti a divorce, 'cause that's all she'll want from me now. At least they'd still have a house to live in."

Andrew bowed his head. Three beautiful marriages blown apart in less than two weeks. How had this happened?

* * *

Inside the house, Jeanette paced the bathroom floor, alternately blowing her nose and splashing cold water on her red, swollen eyelids. Halting abruptly in front of the mirror, she scowled at her reflection. "You aren't Susan, and you never were," she accused herself aloud. "So why do you keep trying to be? A lot of good it's done you—and him."

Sitting on the edge of the bathtub, she spent a long, self-indulgent quarter of an hour whimpering piteously under her own scolding. Then she arose, splashed more water on her face, and met her reflection again with a challenging stare. Now that she'd proved she couldn't be Susan, who *was* she going to be?

Like a film clip in soft focus, a memory formed in her mind: her mother, perched on a kitchen chair, comforting her after a horrific audition for the elite choir in high school. "So you're not Beverly Sills. It doesn't matter. She has her God-given set of gifts, and you have yours. Personally, I like it better when you use your own gifts." A second, more sharply defined memory displaced the first: her father, lecturing her over a tediously difficult math assignment and advising her that "when the going gets tough, the tough get going."

Now was the time to find out what she was really made of. Squaring her jaw, she spoke aloud again. "I'm tough," she announced to her reflection. Then, pulling her car keys from her pants pocket, she added, "And I'm going."

CHAPTER 11
Consequences

Andrew couldn't recall having had a worse day in years. The staff meeting dragged on interminably, focusing on matters that had no bearing on his work or projects. He spent the time drafting apologies to Jeanette on his legal pad while he worried about how Pete was faring at the police station. He was the first out the door when the meeting finally ended and had dialed home on his cell phone before he made it even two strides down the corridor. Thank goodness he had remembered to pick it up from the kitchen table before turning into Mr. Hyde this morning! But there was no answer. He dialed Jeanette's cell phone and got her voice mail; evidently she had turned her phone off. He next dialed Gina's number; she had not seen Jeanette that day, and Pete was "off to some tobaccofest, no doubt." He didn't disillusion her.

Every fifteen minutes he redialed the home phone and Jeanette's cell number. There was no change in either. By ten o'clock he was nearly frantic. He didn't dare call Gina again for fear of arousing her ever-ready suspicions. He called Fiona, the twins, their wives, and Mark; none of them had seen Jeanette. He managed to sound casual enough to avoid alarming them, but they would certainly become alarmed if he called them back. He was ready to leave work and start looking for her, but he had no idea of where to look. Where would a distraught woman with no home or family go if not to her friends?

He redialed steadily all morning, to no avail. He left message after pleading message on her voice mail, hoping that she might pick them up. She didn't. Unable to concentrate, he was reduced to cleaning out his files and rearranging his desk in between pacing and redialing. He would have clocked out in a heartbeat if he'd had any idea where to go. Part of him held to the slim hope that she might not be aware that her cell phone was off, that she might be on her way to visit him at work, to bring him the lunch he had forgotten to bring with him in the midst of this morning's disaster. He gave that notion up at about one o'clock and, in desperation, resolved to call the police. Much though he dreaded hearing Chief Ridley's voice chastising him for spouse abuse and harboring a known criminal, he *had* to know where Jeanette was.

His cell phone was in his hand when his supervisor burst in, breathlessly announcing that a Trojan had entered the computer server and was systematically destroying all the files from Andrew's last project. He was needed now to stop it. Andrew had never been prone to using profanities himself, but he had heard quite a number of them used around the base, and a few of the milder ones entered his mind briefly as he followed his supervisor at a run.

* * *

Jeanette sat at the computer, wiping tears of gratitude from her face with a soggy tissue, thankful that she had chosen a workstation tucked away in a corner. What had happened this morning was, she told herself, nothing to do with luck. It was purely and simply a direct endowment of grace from heaven. She longed to share this news with someone and keenly regretted having forgotten to pick up her cell phone before leaving home.

She read again the newly printed family group sheet in her hand and shook her head. This was why she had persisted in including all generations back to Thomas and Mary Barnes in her quest for Irene's ancestry. It had not made sense, and ultimately it had not helped Mark reclaim his lost fiancée. But it had restored the self-confidence that had been draining steadily from her ever since she had first allowed herself to consider marrying Andrew. Should she borrow the center's phone and call him at work with the news? But he would be in the cafeteria now, she realized, glancing at her watch. He'd forgotten his sack lunch this morning, which had been lying on the kitchen table beside the plate he had never sat down to this morning.

A hand came to rest on her shoulder. "Have you found anything good?" asked an older woman who volunteered at the center.

Jeanette turned. "Oh, Jane, look what I just found!" she exclaimed, pointing at the family group sheet. "The oldest son, William Barnes, is my third great-grandfather from Wiltshire, England. He joined the Church in 1842 with his wife, and they and their children immigrated to Nauvoo in 1843. They came west by wagon during the exodus and ended up in Logan, Utah. I knew about all that, but look down here at his youngest brother, Thomas. *He* joined the Church twenty-two years later and came west with his wife and son in one of the down-and-back companies! They settled in Centerville. I never realized that another of the family had joined the Church."

Jane smiled. "That *is* exciting! So you have a whole pool of cousins here in Utah that you never knew about."

"And look at this," Jeanette commanded, flourishing another printed sheet, this one a six-generation descendancy chart with two names highlighted.

Jane scrutinized it closely and laughed delightedly. "You're related to Susan McCammon? Let's see—six generations . . . that would make you . . ."

"Fifth cousins," Jeanette beamed. "I just calculated it."

"That's wonderful. So you're fifth cousin to the stake president as well. Did you come looking for this?"

"No, I never even suspected it. I was researching a family problem from just one generation back, but for some reason I kept feeling that I ought to take a closer look at Thomas's family."

"Is all the information authentic?"

"It is. The Barnes brothers' hometown was Steeple Ashton in Wiltshire, and someone has the mid-1800s parish register microfilms on loan right here at the center. I was able to verify everything. See here?" She brandished two more photocopies with marginal notes highlighted. "The parish clerk even noted beside William's name that he'd joined a 'deluded sect' and moved to America. And then by Thomas's entry, he wrote, *Idem Gmus*, 'the same as William.' But nobody made the connection, probably because the Latin abbreviation for William didn't make sense to someone who didn't know the whole story."

Jane tittered. "I love it when the clerks bad-mouth the early converts. It makes verification so much easier. What will you do from here?"

"I think I'll spend a little more time filling in Thomas's descendancy lines. Maybe I can contact a few cousins. Then I guess I'll go back to the problem that brought me here in the first place."

"Well, this is a find to celebrate. Here, have a wintergreen Life Saver. It's on the house."

As Jane walked away to greet an arriving patron, Jeanette recalled with exhilaration the sudden flood of warmth that had bathed her as she'd highlighted Susan's name on the descendancy chart. *Susan and I aren't opponents at all. We're family; we're a team*, she thought.

A new thought entered her mind, as clearly formed as if someone had whispered it into her ear. It sent tingles through her. *We were a team before time began.*

Jeanette fumbled through her purse. It was time for another tissue.

* * *

The Trojan was a serious one, Andrew found. It was targeting his actual files and not merely the file directories. He believed in double backups, fortunately, and had the entire project stored on a set of read-only CDs. Still, it was alarming to see his carefully filed labors disrupted in this way. The Trojan had to be stopped. Then he could restore his files to the server from the backups in a marathon session that would take the rest of the day or longer.

But even as he dealt with the crisis, he hoped for a telephone call that would relieve his distress about Jeanette. He nearly did curse aloud—mildly—when he realized that he had left his cell phone in his office. Now the best he could hope for would be a message from her when he finally got away from this catastrophe.

* * *

Casually, Pete sauntered toward the huge tree in the Roylances' backyard. After glancing at the house to make sure that he was unobserved, he took hold of the rope ladder dangling from the treehouse door and nimbly scaled it. Practice had made perfect. Not even the collapsible cooler hanging from one wrist hampered him. The basket elevator had been useful when he was still hauling Andrew's laptop up here, but his ladder skills were flawless now. All the kids had gone to the nearby water park today, and here he could be alone to meditate on the strange turn that his life had taken.

Sitting with his back to the tree's massive trunk, he felt the familiar urge for a cigarette, followed almost immediately by the impulse to retch. With a wry smile, he opened the cooler, took out a stalk of celery, and bit into it, disciplining himself to chew it slowly and thoroughly. Once the chunk of celery in his mouth was reduced to a wad of juiceless, stringy cud, he forced himself to swallow it, nearly losing his lunch as a consequence. Hannah's remedy for thumb-sucking was a winner. In no more than another week, he estimated, the very thought of tobacco would have him vomiting.

Hannah hadn't used celery, of course. Her pet aversion was green peppers. But, Pete reflected with some satisfaction, it had taken her nearly a month to break her habit. His choice of celery added a gross texture to unpalatable taste in a sort of double-whammy. In consequence, his entire system was very quickly losing all desire for tobacco. And once he had kicked that habit, he could kick the collapsible cooler and its dreaded contents into the next county.

He took another bite and let his thoughts wander to the last time he had choked down a stick of this wretched excuse for food, just prior to his visit to the police station this morning. Once it was gone, he had walked into the station expecting not to see the light of day again until he was extradited to Chicago. It had been almost a relief to think of being locked away from Marti when she discovered that her home was gone and that her husband had been living a lie for the past several years. Approaching the officer on duty, he had stuck out his hands for the cuffs, stating, "I'm Pietro Locatelli. I surrender."

The officer had grinned broadly. "So you're Pete, are you? I can see that we're going to get along just great. Hey, chief," he had called. "Your man's here. You were right—I didn't even have to make an appointment."

Chief Ridley had come from his office immediately, his hand extended. To Pete's surprise, he'd been holding neither a pistol nor a pair of handcuffs, but a piece of paper. "Hey, Mr. Locatelli. We just finished printing out a revision of your résumé. Take a look at it, will you, and make sure we didn't add any errors? I'd like to fax it to a few of the other chiefs in the area and then get it to the commissioner right away. If he'll clear it, we could have you hired by the end of this week."

If the building had fallen in on him, Pete couldn't have been more floored. "Hired? For what?"

"Gang-unit consultant, of course. For the whole region. We can't afford to hire you for just our department, see, so I had to persuade some other chiefs to spring for some of your salary. But they're all for it. When I told 'em how you had those punks pegged just from readin' their graffiti, they started forkin' over like you wouldn't believe. You're exactly what we need around here."

For a moment Pete had been tempted to accept the curveball as it was thrown to him. But he had suddenly realized that he didn't have the nerve to disappoint Marti again. Taking a last deep breath, he'd blurted out the truth, the whole truth, and nothing but. "Chief, I don't wanna bust your bubble, but you're talkin' to the wrong guy, ya know. I'm in organized crime, and they've probably got a warrant out for me in Chicago this minute."

The officer on duty had laughed uproariously. The chief, grinning also, had punched him on the arm playfully. "Hey, I hate to disappoint you, but you haven't got a warrant and prob'ly never will. Sure, you're a Locatelli and all, but the Chicago force has been trackin' you for years, and they say you're the cleanest gangster that never was. You've never done anything they could even give you a ticket for, and you don't know enough about the company's inner workings to be a decent informer."

Lounging against the tree's rough trunk, Pete smiled ruefully as he recalled his reaction. "Hey, I've worked in the family business since I was sixteen," he'd begun defensively.

"Yeah, we know about that, too," Chief Ridley had continued. "So we tested out the waters. After we talked to the boys on the force, Sergeant Layton here"—he indicated the still-guffawing officer on duty—"called Locatelli Brothers directly, posin' as a crime boss looking at recruiting you. They told him that you weren't worth his trouble. No hit experience, no racketeering, no laundering, nothing. Just a computer geek."

"Geek!" Pete had exploded. "Those slimy ratfinks! Who do they think—" He'd broken off at that point, partly because the two policemen were laughing too hard to listen to him, but mostly because he'd realized that defending his role as a gangster was insanely counterproductive. As they'd stood there chortling until tears streamed from their eyes, he had suddenly seen the dawning of the new day he'd prayed for.

"Listen—heh!" Chief Ridley had managed through a final snicker, putting an arm around his shoulders. "There are a million real criminals out there that we need our jail space for, 'stead of wastin' it on harmless folks like you. You've got a chance to go straight with no questions asked, draw a decent salary, and do a service for the community. How can bein' a low-level geek in the Locatelli outfit compare with that? And don't worry about knowin' more than you should about them. If they thought you did, they'd have shot you instead of movin' you out of state. What do you say?"

Well, what was there to say, after all?

"If the commissioner offers," Pete had announced after a dazed pause, "I'm in."

Pete gloated over the memory for a moment longer. He wasn't an uneducated, unqualified loser anymore. He was an "urban anthropologist." It had said so, right on the résumé. He could hardly wait to tell the bishop.

Rising, he went to a window and looked out. The view from Locatelli Brothers' seventeenth-floor offices was nothing compared to this. Placid, green backyards ornamented with trees, flowers, and vegetable gardens met his eyes in every direction. Soon, a neighborhood like this would be home, and Chicago would be a distant memory, along with his crime ties—

that is, if the commissioner went along with it. For the first time, he felt a chill of misgiving. *What if the guy doesn't see things the way the chief does? What if he thinks I'm a spy or something?*

A sudden movement caught the corner of his eye and brought him back to the present. Just over that backyard fence—some big, dark fellow, shoveling dirt. He was ugly, too.

Pete moved to another treehouse window for a better look. He'd spent days surveying the neighborhood, trying to discern for himself whether it was as safe and sleepy as it looked and as Gina said it was. He knew nearly everyone in the area by sight now, but this guy didn't belong here. And he acted like he didn't belong, too—he kept looking around as if he was afraid someone would see him. Pete shook his head pityingly. This buzzard definitely wasn't the brightest bulb on the planet. The only two ways into the backyard were on either side of the house, but the dimwit was facing away from the house as he dug, so he had to keep looking over his shoulders. And like most people, he forgot to look up.

Then Pete noticed more motion, between the houses to the left of the one where the guy was digging. He caught a glimpse of two little girls, one dark-haired and one very blond, walking hand in hand toward his right. They acted hesitant, and though they were talking to each other, their voices were too low to carry. Pete had seen the children in this neighborhood enough to know that this was unusual. Most of them ran wherever they went and raised enough ruckus to drown out a fire siren. He maneuvered to get another look at them as they passed in front of the house where the gargoyle was digging.

They appeared and stopped, still talking in those strangely lowered voices. Then, to his horror, they changed direction and disappeared between the houses. They were heading for the backyard, straight into Mr. Ugly's clutches!

Gasping, he looked frantically around the treehouse for something to throw. If he could distract the jerk at the right moment or get him to make some noise, maybe the girls would see or hear him and run before he saw them. His collapsible cooler was the only thing he had, and it didn't pack enough weight to make it past Gina's fence, let alone the forty yards it would have to travel to land anywhere near the guy. By the time he turned back to the window, the damage was done. The two girls rounded the corner and stopped short, frozen in shock, just as the mug turned and saw them.

There was an instant of silence, then the man dropped his shovel and began to growl like a cornered wild animal. He snatched at his belt, and when he raised his hand again, something metallic in his clenched fist glittered coldly in the summer sun. He headed straight for the two children, crouching slightly, his weapon arm raised.

The girls screamed simultaneously and grabbed for each other, backing away instinctively—straight into the corner of the house. There they huddled as if trapped.

Pete did his best. Cupping his hands around his mouth, he bellowed, "Hey, bozo, you've got another witness over here. Get *me* if you can." To the girls he added, "Run, you two. Get outta there!"

Distracted, the man turned toward the voice and, to Pete's relief, panicked. Dropping the metallic whatever-it-was—a knife, Pete judged, since it was apparently no threat to a distant target—he grabbed a rock and hurled it at the treehouse. Automatically, Pete dodged away from the window, but the rock didn't even hit the treehouse wall. Judging from the sound of crunching foliage, the missile landed somewhere in the middle of Gina's impeccably manicured vegetable garden.

"Pathetic," Pete muttered. If it had been any of the boys back in Chicago, they'd have nailed him before he could have moved. Of course, the boys would have been armed to the teeth with semiautomatics and so wouldn't have bothered with rocks. Not for the first time, Pete considered the advantages of living away from his kinfolk.

He peered around the corner again and saw, to his dismay, that the girls were still visible in the backyard. The blond one stood still, crying in terror, while the dark one, equally terrified, yanked desperately at her friend's clothing. *She musta got snagged on something,* Pete thought wildly. Their assailant had retrieved his knife and was heading toward them again.

Cupping his hands again, he yelled, "Hey, ya dork! Think I can't pick you out of a police lineup? Think again."

The assailant turned to shake a fist at Pete and call out a threat in some unrecognizable language. It was long enough for the cavalry to arrive.

Around the right corner of the house dashed a large, red dog, followed by a patrolman running flat out. Simultaneously, around the left corner of the house and past the two girls came another large dog, the color of dark chocolate, dragging a harried-looking man of middle age.

The patrolman called out some indistinct command, and both dogs leaped for the ugly man at the same instant. True to its training, the K-9 went straight for the weapon arm and latched onto the wrist with a set of fangs that, even from a distance, looked impressive. The other dog, untrained but with no less zeal, went for the opposite ankle. Both pulled backward, snarling ferociously, stretching the hapless assailant between them like a wishbone from a Thanksgiving turkey. Pete leaned against the wooden window frame, enjoying the spectacle.

It was over in moments. The criminal was begging for mercy even before he lost his balance and tumbled to the ground. The patrolman produced handcuffs and had them on the guy's wrists almost before the K-9 had let go. It took a moment to get the dark dog to relinquish the ankle, but eventually it did so and turned to lick the blond girl's face soothingly.

Pete headed for the door and the rope ladder. He knew the procedure. He'd be on hand to give his eyewitness report before the patrolman had finished reading the assailant his Miranda rights.

CHAPTER 12
Redemption

Stretching at her computer, Jeanette glanced at her watch. It was nearing two o'clock. Andrew was sure to be back in his office by now. Guiltily, she recalled how poorly she had behaved when sending him off to work. She'd better begin her phone call with an abject apology. Still, she hoped that he would be as delighted with her discovery as she had been, that he would somehow understand what it meant to her, even though she could barely begin to explain it to herself.

She was on her way to the phone on the reception desk when a tug came at her sleeve. "Sister McCammon?"

She turned to see a shy young woman cradling something in her arms.

"Do you remember me? I'm Cyndi Blake."

"Of course I do. You were at the family history activity last week, weren't you?"

"Yes. When I couldn't find you at your house, I thought of trying to find you here." She held out an old, battered book bound in speckled cardboard. "I showed my mom that family group sheet from Parowan, and she gave me this. I think it might help with the problem we were working on."

Taking the book, Jeanette examined it with interest. "A journal? Whose was it?"

"My grandmother's. Her name was Charlotte Snow Newman."

Jeanette's mouth flew open.

"I'd stay and show it to you, but I'm on the way to work. We marked the places that might be useful," Cyndi added, indicating a ragged line of torn sticky notes along the edges of the pages. "Mom says you can keep it until Sunday and copy whatever you need."

"Thank you, Cyndi," Jeanette said, suddenly breathless. "I'll be very careful with it."

The girl smiled. "I know you will." She turned and left.

Sinking down into the nearest chair, Jeanette opened to the title page and began to read. The handwriting was small but neat and legible. *Journal of Charlotte S. Newman, 1950–1951.* Hastily, she turned to the first sticky note.

August 24. Our honeymoon is over. We have barely settled into our little home, and now another is coming to join us. If it were a baby of our own, I would be overjoyed, but this is not at all the same. Cleve's sister Linda will be arriving in a few days. I have consented, reluctantly, to this invasion of our intimacy because of poor Cleve. The death of his sister Phyllis in such sordid circumstances struck him very hard, and he blames himself for not having worked with her more to maintain her testimony of the gospel. Because of this, he feels obliged to help Linda out of the bad situation she is fleeing. I pray that I will be able to contain my resentment and be of some service to my sister-in-law.

This sounded definitive but not promising for Mark's hopes. With some trepidation, Jeanette turned to the next sticky note.

September 18. Linda's physical condition is improving. She has also given up much of the moping in her room that filled her first few weeks with us. Yesterday evening, she opened up for the first time and told us about the young man who brought her to this state. After hearing her story, we cannot help but rejoice that he is gone from her life. Marriage to such a brazenly evil person would be intolerable for her. But though she realizes this with her head, her heart has not yet recovered. We have urged her to attend church with us, but she continues to refuse.

Jeanette sighed impatiently and wished that Charlotte had been a little less delicate in speaking of "Linda's physical condition." Resolutely, she turned to the next marker and read on.

September 26. Time is working its magic, and Linda is becoming quite a pleasant and useful addition to our household. She takes her turn at cooking, keeps the mending up very well, and handles the washing machine much better than I do. She has at last consented to attend church with us, in spite of the gossip and finger-pointing that she is sure her appearance will provoke. Considering her situation, this is quite a natural reaction. I pray that the good sisters of our community will withhold judgment and extend to her the love and understanding that she needs.

This was getting worse with each entry. Jeanette sought temporary refuge in a cup of cold water before continuing. But, she resolved sternly as she took up the journal again, this time she would read until the truth came out, come what may.

* * *

"Well, that should about do it," Patrolman Justin Price concluded, folding his notebook shut. "We'll be in touch if we need anything more from you on this case. You're a very observant witness, sir."

"Glad to help," Pete answered, relishing how great it felt to be surrounded by a swarm of police and not to be nervous in the least.

"And I'm sure that Chief Ridley will want to thank you personally for your quick thinking," Justin added. "He loves all his daughters, but I've always suspected that he has a soft spot for Bethany here." He indicated the dark-haired girl who, her recent ordeal seemingly forgotten, was frolicking with the red Irish setter, whose name, Pete had learned, was Patrick Seamus O'Hooligan—Paddy for short.

Pete demurred modestly. "I was too far away to be much help, ya know? Good thing you and Paddy were out walking at just the right time—and this gentleman with Laddie."

The middle-aged owner of the big brown dog was still mopping his forehead with a handkerchief. "That's more exercise than I've had in years," he admitted to the officer who had just finished taking his report. "If you've heard all you need from me, constable, I think I'll take Laddie home and lie down for a while."

Far from being worn down by the excitement, Pete felt energized. As the police were taking down their final notes on the scene of the incident, he helped the blond-haired girl—a pretty little thing, though not very talkative—to gather up the scattered wildflowers she had been carrying when the grave robber had attacked. For robbery, apparently, was exactly what the guy had been up to. The corpse Chief Ridley had been talking about the evening before had been buried right here. This poor little foreign kid had simply come over to put flowers on her daddy's grave site, only to find the lowlife jerk who had buried him apparently trying to resurrect the dead man's ID for his own use. Well, he wouldn't be trying that again anytime soon.

Pete threw back his shoulders and swelled his chest with pride. For the second time in three days, he had been actively on the right side of the law. *If I'd known it felt this good,* he told himself, *I'd have done it ages ago, and to heck with the family business.*

* * *

Jeanette gathered up the freshly made photocopies of Charlotte's journal and carefully stowed the original book in her file box. Her cheeks were still damp from tears of gratitude. *I've got to think of some special way to thank Cyndi,* she thought. *She's restored Mark and Alyssa to an eternity of happiness. And I think*

Irene owes her a big debt as well. Smiling, she again read the pages with the journal entries that had first begun to unravel the problem.

October 10. For the second time, our home has become a refuge for a girl in trouble. Poor little Lydia arrived from Boston two days ago. She is an orphan, the foster daughter of the parents-in-law of Cleve's brother Harold, and has been sent to us to conceal from their high-society friends in the East the fact that she is with child. She is but sixteen years old, no more than a child herself, and about to become a mother. It makes me sick at heart. Of the baby's father, Lydia will say only that she does not expect to see him again.

Sad though all this is, nothing has done so much good for Linda. Her own problems have paled in comparison, for Lydia is the embodiment of the situation Linda might have been in herself if heaven had not intervened. When Linda's drunken brute of a boyfriend tried to force himself on her, she succeeded in escaping him with her purity intact. The bruises on her face and arms have very nearly faded away now, and soon she may succeed in putting the whole terrible incident behind her. But Lydia's predicament will become more visible as time goes on, and her life will never be the same.

Linda's sympathetic concern won Lydia's confidence almost immediately. The two have become fast friends and spend nearly every waking moment in each other's company. I cannot help but think that the Lord has had a hand in bringing these two girls together so that they may help each other to heal from the tragic experiences that have marred their young lives . . .

October 19. Our two girls have become a sisterhood. They are Linnie and Lyddie, and it is impossible to speak of one without mentioning the other. I would have felt quite left out, but they have dubbed me Lottie and insist that I am one of them. I feel honored. They help me with the housework, and we laugh the days away in each other's company. Cleve jokes that he is quite the odd man out. To think that I resented the coming of these darling girls as an intrusion! May God forgive my foolishness . . .

October 30. I find that I have something in common with Lydia. This I discovered to my great joy this morning, when I lost my breakfast at about the same time she lost hers. Her baby will be born some three months before ours, and she considers herself quite the woman of experience as she lectures me about remedies for nausea and the foods that settle best in a queasy stomach. Linda is content to soak in this useful information for future use . . .

Jeanette's smile faded and her eyes misted as she read on.

February 23. Lyddie's baby will be born in about eight weeks. Cleve and I have spoken to her long and earnestly about the future, and I believe that we have finally persuaded her to choose a course that will benefit both her and her child. She has progressed from wanting to keep the baby and raise it herself to wanting us to adopt it. We are humbled that she would trust us to do this for her, but the adoption counselors assure us that it is healthiest for all involved if the birth mother and child are completely separated and no contact exists between them. In this way, the child can be brought up with no sense of conflict over who his or her parents are. Lyddie does not entirely agree with this, but she is willing to refrain from contact with the child if we will maintain contact with the adoptive parents and reassure her now and then that her child is being raised well.

Cleve suggested my sister's friends as parents who could give her child a comfortable and loving home. Her first question about them was whether they are members of our church. This surprised us all. Lyddie has attended church with Linnie and us out of fellowship and seems to like the other members of our ward, but she has never shown any particular interest in the doctrines and has never asked any questions. She tells us that she wants a home for her child such as she has known with us. According to her, family life among the wealthy in Boston is more like living among strangers in a grand hotel. The wealth, she says, can never replace the love that she feels in our home . . .

April 21. Lyddie's baby daughter was born this morning at about 9:30. Both are doing well. Linnie was their first visitor and will most likely stay until the nurses send her home for the night. We were half afraid that once she saw the infant, Lyddie would revert to her former decision. She is tearful but determined to follow through with what will benefit the child most. When I think what it must cost her, I want to cry too.

The adoption service workers have contacted the parents-to-be, and they are ecstatic. They have a room already furnished and filled with toys and baby equipment. Tomorrow they will shop for clothing in shades of pink, and in two days they will arrive to claim their daughter. This will give poor Lyddie very little time to enjoy the child she has carried all these months.

Linnie is a tower of strength, offering encouragement and comfort. She was the one who insisted that Lyddie be introduced to the adoption workers as her sister and Cleve's. In the gospel sense, this is true, of course, and Linnie maintains that a sister-in-law's sister is close enough to be a sister in fact. A rumor is circulating in the community that Lyddie has a husband who is missing in action in the war in Korea. When I confronted Linnie, she claimed that the good sisters in the ward jumped to that conclusion themselves and that she has played along to keep Lyddie from becoming the subject of hurtful gossip. I can't deny that I probably would have done the same . . .

April 24. Lyddie's daughter and her new parents have left for their home in northern Utah. We have shed many tears today, but we all feel assured that this sweet little baby has every prospect for a happy life. As a final gift, the new parents offered to let Lyddie name her child. She declined. But when they proposed the name Irene, Lyddie wept again and told them that she would have selected that very name; it was the name of her favorite nursemaid as she was growing up in Boston. We all see this as a witness from God that His will has been done . . .

May 27. Another day of tears. Lyddie has left us to return to her foster home in Boston. This has always been the plan of her foster parents, but her personal plans have changed since her experience *with us. She plans to continue her schooling and to get a university degree so that she will always be able to support herself and accomplish some good in the world. She is no longer content to be idly dependent on her foster parents' money. She has assured us that she will always stay in touch with us.*

Linnie has consented to stay on until the end of summer to be of service to Cleve and me when our child is born. I am deeply grateful. The house already seems half-empty without Lyddie, and if Linnie were to leave, I would be alone for most of the day. Linnie has grown so competent and loving and selfless! It seems strange to admit it, but I will always remember with thanks the day that her so-called boyfriend beat her in his drunken rage. By driving her away, he spared her a life of misery and allowed her to become a mentor in Lyddie's life and a blessing in mine. I have every confidence that she will never again lose sight of the gospel that has become so precious to her.

Cleve's decision to bring Linnie into our home has healed him of deep wounds as well. He seems finally to have come to terms with his own dismal youth and his guilt over not having remained at home to strengthen his sisters. I can read the pride and love in his eyes each time he looks at her. It is another evidence of our Heavenly Father's power to turn evil to His own good purposes for the sake of His beloved children.

Jeanette could breathe a hearty amen to that. Now, except for a few loose ends, she had a complete vindication of Susan's mother and an authoritative lineage for Irene. She glanced at the clock; Andrew would probably be en route home now, in rush-hour traffic. There would be time for that call to Cyndi's mother before she could hope to reach him.

* * *

By six o'clock, the Trojan had been found and defeated, and Andrew had salvaged the files. He entered his office at a run, grabbed his cell phone and briefcase, and checked his office phone for messages. None. He checked his cell phone for messages on his way to the car. None. If the traffic cooperated, he might have a chance to look in at home before heading to the meetinghouse for the evening's prospective missionary meeting with the ward's young men. He hadn't had a spare minute to plan what he might say to them. He would simply have to hope that the Spirit would direct him.

The traffic didn't cooperate. While stalled in a ten-minute traffic jam, he tried again to phone Jeanette. There was no answer at home, and her cell phone was still turned off. One by one, he dialed each of his children. Neither of the twins had heard from her. Fiona and Spencer—who was his ward's mission leader—were in a missionary discussion, and Mark was at his night class. Frustrated, he slapped the phone shut and thumped the steering wheel. Where was his wife? How far away had he driven her with that hideously insensitive remark this morning? What could he do to find her?

Andrew arrived at the meeting with half a minute to spare. To both his whispered inquiries during the opening announcements, Steve responded with a politely puzzled smile; Pete was fine and spending the evening at home, and no one at the Roylance house had seen or heard from Jeanette that day. Ignoring his own stern directive to his bishopric, Andrew deliberately left his cell phone on during the meeting, hoping against hope that she would call. She didn't.

* * *

Jeanette glanced at the clock and compressed her lips in annoyance. Thanks to her total elation at the results of her phone call to Cyndi's mother and her subsequent research, she had succeeded in locating nearly every bit of verification. But she had missed the entire window of time in which she might have contacted Andrew before his meeting with the young men. There was no point in calling him now; he would have turned off his cell phone, and leaving a message on matters so important would be more frustrating than beneficial. But with only three phone calls left to make, she might as well take care of them now and drive to the meetinghouse to meet Andrew and tell him the news. The sooner he knew about her day's work, the better.

* * *

To his great relief, Andrew found that the Spirit did fill his mouth when he arose on schedule to address the young men, even though he felt like the most miserable excuse for a bishop that the world had ever seen. His message was concise—which was probably good, given the attention span of his audience and the amount of time already taken by the Young Men presidency in their portion of the program. By the time the closing prayer had concluded, it was almost nine o'clock. Following a brief, whispered request to Steve to field any questions or comments for him, he skirted the growing throng at the refreshment table and escaped through the doors to his car. He had the Beastie started and in gear before the door was shut, and he might have set a speed record in getting it out of the parking lot and onto the road that led to home.

His heart contracted painfully as he pulled into the driveway. No porch light and no interior lights. *Maybe she's in the bedroom reading,* he told himself, knowing that it was a comforting lie. He made it to the front door with a single flying leap up the porch stairs, jammed his key into the lock, and shoved the door open with a haste that sent it banging against the wall.

The room was dark. The hallway was dark. There was no aroma of cooking dinner. The only sound was the faint purring of the refrigerator from the direction of the kitchen. He switched on the overhead light and stampeded into the living room, scanning the area for a note or a clue of any kind. He had just time enough to verify that there was none before the light blinked out, leaving him once again in darkness. Simultaneously, the refrigerator gurgled into silence. Power failure.

The extinction of the light was painfully symbolic. Andrew stood still in the shadows and let the tears gather in his eyes. She really was gone. He had let himself put everything and everyone else in creation before her, and now she was gone. What had Russ told him when he was set apart? *Schedule your family time with an indelible pencil—twice if you have to, but get it in.* He hadn't done it, and now Jeanette was gone. How under heaven could he go on now?

At first he thought he was imagining the delicate sound of footfalls behind him. Then came the softly hummed melody of "Dancing in the Dark" in a relaxed, mezzo-soprano register, and his pounding heart nearly stopped. Wheeling toward the door, he saw a tall, slender form framed in the open doorway, with moonlight glinting off her hair. The humming broke off as the figure advanced toward him. "Care to dance, bishop?" asked a light, tender, gently teasing voice.

Andrew moved toward her. Before he drowned in this overwhelming tsunami of conflicting emotions, he had to hold Jeanette in his arms again. She entered them easily and swayed to her own renewed humming. He shuffled his feet ineptly, following her lead as a limp frond of seaweed follows the gentle flow of its nurturing ocean. For a moment, there was nothing in the world but the two of them and this glorious moment.

She interrupted her own humming once again to press a kiss against his lips. "We need to brush up on your dancing. You're going to need it soon. We have a wedding to celebrate."

"Are we getting married again?" he asked heedlessly. "Not that I mind, of course," he added hastily. "I'd marry you any number of times."

Her laugh was liquid gold in the silver of the moonlight. "Once for time and eternity will cover us, I think. No, this time, you'll be the father of the groom."

Andrew stopped shuffling. "You mean Mark? Then you've found something?" He hugged her joyfully, lifting her off her feet. "Have you told him yet?"

"I haven't gotten hold of him. I forgot my cell phone this morning, and I've been regretting it all day. And speaking of this morning," she diverged, pulling away from him slightly to look him in the face, "will you forgive me, dearest? I wasn't my best self, I'm afraid. In fact, I wasn't myself at all, and I'm so sorry."

"Forgiven and forgotten. The big issue is whether *you* can forgive *me* for being such a complete Philistine."

"You didn't tell me anything that I didn't need to hear. I was so busy trying to be Susan that I couldn't be any worthwhile help to you. I forgive anything you want me to forgive, but I don't want to forget what this day has taught me. Oh, Andrew, I've got so much to tell you!"

"I want to hear every syllable of it. Listen, we need to eat, and we can't fix any food with the power off. How about if I take you to the finest restaurant in the valley just as soon as we've talked to Mark?"

"I'd love it," she replied, "but we'll have to make do with Dutch's Diner for tonight. We're supposed to meet Alyssa and her parents there at nine thirty."

"At Dutch's? I thought it closed at nine thirty."

"It does. Alyssa's on duty as the receptionist until then. When I told Dutch what it was about, he agreed to give us an exclusive late-night booking and to make sure that Alyssa doesn't leave before we arrive. He said he'd order her to wash dishes if he had to. But we need to get hold of Mark. He should be home from his night class by now."

Andrew dialed the number with one hand while holding Jeanette's with the other and then put the phone on speaker as it was ringing. Mark answered in melancholy tones on the fourth ring, but at least he answered. "Mark? It's Dad. Never mind about heating anything up for dinner. We're taking you out. Can you meet us at Dutch's at nine thirty?"

There was a long pause. Mark's distraught voice finally broke the silence. "Dad, please don't do this to me."

Instantly Andrew realized how clumsily he had broached the invitation. "Mark," he answered contritely, "there's no way I'd ask it unless I was certain that this could be the best night of your life—so far."

Another pause. The voice that responded was almost unrecognizably different and filled with tense, wondering hope. "Nan's found something?"

"I've found something," Jeanette confirmed. "Your mom and Alyssa's are definitely not sisters, and I've got conclusive proof."

A crash sounded through the phone speaker, as if a kitchen chair had just been knocked over onto a linoleum floor. "I'll be there!" Mark shouted. In the same moment, the overhead light flickered on.

If that wasn't an omen, Andrew had never experienced one.

There wasn't time for more than a minute or two of renewed dancing before they had to leave for Dutch's. "Let's take Daisy," Jeanette suggested casually as Andrew pulled the front door shut. "All my notes and documents are in her. Besides, I think the Beastie could use a rest after the way you drove home just now."

"You saw me?" Andrew asked, mortified.

"I followed you," Jeanette corrected. "I pulled into the parking lot by the south entrance as you shot out the north entrance. Shall I drive this time?"

"Maybe you should," he admitted.

The meeting at Dutch's went flawlessly. The three McCammons arrived at the same moment, with the elder Jarvises no more than half a minute behind them. The restaurant owner, a stout, gray-eyed man with nondescript, thinning hair and a magnificent handlebar mustache, met the party at the door himself and, with a dramatic air of secrecy, led them to a secluded table set for six. "Alyssa is in the kitchen," he announced with a trace of Dutch accent. "I'll send her out right away. I hope you will all enjoy today's special. It's on the house."

Del and Irene Jarvis were as pleasant as ever, but with more than a hint of wariness to their manner, as if they suspected that a very highly powered sales pitch was in the works. Andrew could hardly blame them. Nor could he blame Alyssa when she suddenly rounded the corner and turned white upon seeing Mark. But Jeanette was in her element.

"Alyssa, I hope you kept those wedding announcements," she began, "because I've found your mom's birth mother, and she wasn't related to Mark."

Alyssa sank weakly into the chair that Mark hastily placed for her. But within a minute, she was standing with the rest of them, her face flushed with happiness, reading avidly over Irene's shoulder from an old, handwritten book bound in speckled cardboard. Before the day's specials arrived, Irene's reserve had vanished, and she was tearfully embracing Mark while Del pounded him on the back and Alyssa hopped impatiently in the background, awaiting her turn.

When it came, it was electric. As Mark took Alyssa into his arms, it was as if the room filled with light. Sounds seemed hushed, and Andrew felt almost as if he had entered a holy place. As the two young people kissed fervently and clung tightly to each other, tears flowing freely, he could feel the presence of Susan beside him. His son—*their* son—had undergone an Abrahamic test and had passed it. This boded well for the future of his family to come, now and in the eternities. On his other side, Jeanette was wiping tears of her own and glowing as if she were illuminated from within.

The clearing of a throat from somewhere behind Andrew broke the silence. Turning his head, he saw five young people, each bearing a tray, beaming and nudging each other. In their midst stood Dutch, holding a sixth tray and looking as benevolent and fatherly as Andrew felt. Mark and Alyssa, suddenly aware that they had become an exhibition, broke apart and blushed becomingly rosy.

Congratulations filled the air as the two families reseated themselves and the servers placed meals in front of them. After a heartfelt prayer of thanks and a blessing on the food, they ate as Jeanette summed up her conversation with the woman who had supplied her with the journal.

"Her name is Lyndia Blake, and she's the oldest daughter of Cleve and Charlotte. They named her after both Lydia and Linda. She'd thought that she might be related to Russ Newman but wasn't sure how—I guess because Cleve and Linda had become so estranged from their brothers that the next generation had lost all contact. But she says that she never knew the whole story until her mother died and left her this journal. Her daughter Cyndi hadn't even read the journal until yesterday, but she recognized her grandparents' names at the family history activity last week and took home the family group sheet to show to her mother.

"Lyndia told me that Lydia's foster parents, Lewis and Frances Peabody, had taken her in as a foundling because Frances sponsored a charity for a local foundlings' asylum. Lydia was sort of the poster child. They never formally adopted her because they wanted the family fortune to go to their only biological child, Adele. But Adele was rather headstrong, and she eloped with Linda's brother Harold against her parents' wishes. The scandal of her daughter running off with a penniless young Westerner of no social standing just about destroyed Frances, socially and emotionally.

"Harold was probably trying to ingratiate himself with his parents-in-law when he arranged to place Lydia in Cleve's care. It didn't work very well, though. By the time Lydia went home again, Adele's parents had already pressured her into divorcing him. Harold drowned in Boston harbor in 1952, and whether it was an accident or suicide has never really been resolved. Adele eventually remarried someone about twice her age, but wealthy and more to her parents' taste. She's been a widow for many years now and is very reclusive. She sends donations to lots of arts foundations and charitable causes, but she never leaves her home.

"Lydia never married. After she went back to Boston, she finished high school and began applying to universities. She graduated from Princeton, earned advanced degrees from Yale, and eventually joined the faculty at Carnegie-Mellon University in Pittsburgh. She enjoyed a long and distinguished career there and became the only faculty member in the university's history to win the major student-nominated teaching award three times. When she died in 1999, the university canceled classes on the day of her funeral so that all students and faculty could attend. All this comes from the obituary in the school newspaper; I had it faxed to me this afternoon. Here's a copy."

Irene reverently took the proffered paper from Jeanette. "What a wonderful heritage," she breathed emotionally. "I only wish that I could have met her."

"There's more," Jeanette said quietly. "Lydia did join the Church in the fall of 1960. She was one of the first people to be baptized in the font of the first meetinghouse the Church constructed in Pittsburgh. She was serving as the education counselor in the Relief Society presidency of the Pittsburgh Second Ward when she died. In her last letter to Cleve and Charlotte Newman, she requested to be sealed to them as their daughter." Jeanette paused to let this intriguing bit of information sink in and then continued. "In view of the uncertainty of her parentage, the First Presidency granted the request. The sealing took place in the Saint George Temple in 2001, with Lyndia as proxy for Lydia."

Irene wrinkled her forehead with concentration. "Then . . . my birth mother is Susan's cousin, according to the sealing line?"

"Yes. And once Mark and Alyssa are married, you and your birth mother will be second cousins by marriage, according to the sealing line."

Irene's eyes widened, and she smiled, but before she could respond, Dutch reappeared, flanked again by his kitchen staff, bearing a luscious-looking chocolate bundt cake drizzled with thin white icing and garnished with red grapes. Further discussion was suspended as the staff burst into a semblance of song about the pending wedding. It was apparently an adaptation of the regular birthday salute and sounded as if it had been composed by Charles Ives, but it was enough to shift the focus of the gathering back to its original subject.

"Actually," Alyssa admitted shyly, "I did keep the wedding announcements. I just couldn't bring myself to throw them away. And, Mom, Dad," she confessed, "every time I thought of phoning to cancel all the arrangements, I couldn't do it. I knew I'd start crying on the phone. I was planning to do it tomorrow."

Mark squeezed her hand gently. "And I never called the real estate agent to cancel our home purchase—for the same reason."

Irene smiled mistily. "Well, my dears," she told them, "I can't say a word. I couldn't bring myself to phone the temple to cancel the sealing appointment either. As far as the rest of the world knows, nothing ever happened to change your plans. How about if we put those announcements in the mail first thing tomorrow morning?"

Del leaned forward. "Better yet, I'll take them to the night slot at the post office as soon as we get home. And I think we'd better let the family know right now." He drew his cell phone from his pocket.

This was a cue for Andrew to extract his cell phone and start dialing his other children. With all these simultaneous conversations and best wishes being relayed around the table, there was little opportunity to introduce any new information, but it didn't really matter. After a helping of dessert, Andrew was ready to leave Dutch and his staff a generous tip each and depart with Jeanette for a private celebration of his own.

Andrew drove on the way home, choosing a quiet and roundabout route for its romantic value and taking care that his cell phone was off. As they traveled, Jeanette revealed to him the rest of her findings of that day. "So Susan and I are cousins—not very close ones, but close enough to matter to me," she concluded happily.

Andrew glanced over at her quizzically. "I don't fully understand why it matters to you so much. But since it does, I'm glad that you found it." *Glad is an understatement,* he added to himself. *To be completely truthful, I'm overcome with joy.*

Jeanette bit her lip. "I was just so obsessed with being everything Susan was to you . . ." Her voice trembled and trailed off.

Pulling over on a side road with a magnificent view of the mountains bathed in moonlight, Andrew cut the engine and took both her hands in his. "Jeanette," he pleaded, "you don't need to compare yourself with anyone else. As your bishop, I'm advising you to be yourself and trust yourself. And as your husband, I'm begging you to trust me. You don't have to be like Susan for me to love you. I married Jeanette because I love Jeanette. You and Susan aren't competitors."

Gradually, Jeanette's face relaxed into a tremulous, wondering smile. "That's the feeling I got at the family history center. I felt as if she was telling me that she and I are a team and that we always had been."

"Maybe all three of us have been," Andrew speculated softly, leaning forward to kiss her. And from the way Jeanette melted into his arms, he felt assured that in spite of the absolutely miserable day he had just endured, he was truly forgiven. With all the odds against him, he, the greatest boor in the history of the western world, had at last managed, somehow, to say the right thing.

CHAPTER 13
Family

THE HONEYMOON IS OVER, ANDREW reflected with satisfaction.

He had never expected those words to evoke such contentment. Yet they did. The honeymoon was over, and the marriage had begun.

He had noticed it the moment he had entered the door that evening: Jeanette had rearranged the furniture. Oh, it wasn't blatantly different, of course. But through subtle adjustments of an already comfortable plan, she had begun to give the house a new sort of feeling. It was as if some living organism that had long been in stasis was at last beginning to grow and thrive again.

Dinner, too, was an old favorite with a new twist: Spanish omelets with potatoes, green peppers, red onions, garbanzo beans, and a blend of herbs that he could not quite identify. It was incomparably delicious—the more so because Jeanette seemed perfectly at ease as she watched him taste it. Andrew felt a twinge of guilt as he reflected that he had entirely missed all the tiny cues that would have communicated her overarching anxiety to him well before yesterday morning.

But he wouldn't let it happen again.

For one thing, he had spent his lunch hour with indelible pen in hand, marking every Monday and Friday evening in his planner as family time. For another, he had sent an e-mail message to Todd Mikesell instructing him that those evenings were sacrosanct, in their entirety, for every member of the bishopric except in the direst of emergencies. For a third, he had written in his planner, at the top of each day's entry for a solid month, "Put Jeanette's happiness first today." By then, he reasoned, it would become a firmly entrenched habit. If not, he would fill it in for another month, and another, until it was.

"So remind me," he said aloud as he rose and began to stack the empty dinner dishes for transport to the sink, "what's on the agenda tonight?"

Jeanette stood to help him. "A brief visit to the Roylance house for some notable announcement by Pete, followed by a first lesson with the missionaries and the Ridleys at the Barlow house."

"And," added Andrew, "we leave the Barlows' at seven thirty, come what may. I've already made that clear to all involved."

"Another appointment?" Jeanette asked.

"More of a rendezvous," Andrew replied mysteriously.

Jeanette smiled. "Do I need to change clothes?"

She already looked wonderful in a gray skirt and a silky blouse of the palest pink. Not since Susan had Andrew encountered a woman who looked so vibrantly beautiful in every style and color known to fashion. "Don't change anything. Just be ready for some serious enjoyment."

They drove the Beastie the short distance to the Barlow home to be prepared for a quick getaway, then strolled hand in hand around the block to the Roylance home as Jeanette regaled Andrew with the latest ward news. "Lenka and her mother—her name is Anya, by the way—have really taken well to sewing. Lenka runs the sewing machine, and Anya does the hand stitching and adds embroidery touches. Sister Jantzen has donated her entire supply of patterns, fabric, and sewing supplies to them, so they have enough to set up a small business now."

Andrew grinned. "Maybe there is some merit in my mother's old saying, 'She who dies with the most fabric wins.' It seems to have blessed a few lives this time."

Jeanette's golden laugh was his reward. "And speaking of Sister Jantzen," she continued, "her new bishop has issued her a temple recommend. President Newman may be signing it at this very moment. She's asked me to give her a date and time when you and I and the Roylances can be present at her endowment and sealing to Carl. I've agreed to be her escort." She paused to squeeze his hand. "And she'd like you to act as proxy for Carl."

Andrew was touched. Having him represent her beloved husband in the temple was the highest honor that Dora Jantzen could bestow. "Please tell her that I'd be thrilled. Let's make it the first day that the Roylances have free."

Pete was waiting at the door as they mounted the Roylances' porch stairs. "Good to see you, ya know?" he greeted them with a pair of hearty handshakes. "Go on in and sit down. Two more people still comin'."

Andrew suspected that tonight's big announcement was related to the Locatelli family's future, but he had no idea what it entailed. He had not yet had an opportunity to learn why Pete was not in jail and seemed happier than he had been since Andrew had first met him. Something else about Pete had changed, too, but he couldn't quite put his finger on it.

They walked into the crowded living room and squeezed onto the couch next to Vinnie and Cat. Nearly every chair was full—with dining room chairs jammed into any extra space—and the floor between them was covered with children and young people. Apparently, the entire clan was here. And two more were still coming? Andrew had no idea who they might be.

Marti sat in a recliner beside two vacant dining room chairs, trying not to keep looking at her watch. She nodded curtly in response to Jeanette's greeting, but all she said was, "After all this buildup, whatever he's going to say had better be good."

Andrew looked questioningly over at Steve, seated next to Gina on a smaller couch. His perennial smile had a quizzical cast, and he shrugged his shoulders slightly. Apparently, Pete had tipped his hand to no one.

Half a minute later, Pete ushered in two young men, unmistakably identifiable by their white shirts, ties, short haircuts, and name badges. Marti's jaw dropped.

"Have a seat, elders, and let's begin." Pete spoke briskly, motioning the missionaries toward the empty chairs beside Marti. "Bishop, I've been smoke-free for a full week. How soon can you get the baptismal font filled?"

The room went as silent as if all air had suddenly been vacuumed out of it. Although his eyes were riveted disbelievingly on Pete, Andrew had the vague impression that everyone else was as incredulous as he was. Pete, the focus of all attention, was clearly basking in it, having the time of his life. Suddenly, Andrew realized what had changed about him: he emanated no tobacco odor, fresh or otherwise.

It was Steve who broke the silence. "Pete, this is fantastic news," he remarked, nothing in his manner betraying whether the word *fantastic* as he used it meant "wonderful" or "downright beyond belief." "I, for one, would love to hear the full story. How did you do it?"

"Well, it was Hannah's idea, really," Pete admitted.

Hannah's eyes grew round. "You ate green peppers?"

"Worse than that," he replied, picking up the collapsible cooler and opening it for display.

Gina gave a most unladylike whoop, while her cousins maintained a stunned silence. It contained nothing but a large, half-empty plastic bag of celery sticks next to a bag of half-melted ice.

"Every time a nicotine fit came on me, I'd stave it off with one of these. So now I hate anything to do with smoking as much as I hate you-know-what. Try me out, if you like," Pete invited. "Say *cigar*." He gagged noticeably in response to his own words.

"Tobacco," Vinnie said suddenly, leaning forward. "Cigarette."

Pete retched twice more in quick succession. "Hey, don't get carried away, ya know? I wanna live to get into that water. So whaddaya say, bishop?"

One of the missionaries turned to Andrew, his face shining. "The font fills in about forty-five minutes, bishop," he supplied. "I've timed it."

"And we can set up a baptismal interview right now," his companion added enthusiastically.

Andrew shifted in his seat. "Let's take up this topic in about five minutes," he suggested as diplomatically as possible. "I'd like to hear a little more from Pete about . . . uh . . . recent events."

Pete grinned from ear to ear, the early evening light from the windows glinting off two gold molars. "Clear the air, he means. No problem. Kids," he began, addressing his son and daughter, "you say you like it here. What about if we buy a house and stay?"

The two froze for a mere instant before erupting into cheers. Jake pounded Gianni on the back and gave him a high five while Sarah screeched and hugged the girl—whose name, if Andrew recalled correctly, was Leti.

Andrew cringed a little. He hoped that Pete wasn't ruining his own prospects by neglecting to ask his wife about such an important matter. A glance at Marti showed that she was still in a state of shock. It was a good thing that she had chosen to sit in the recliner.

"Now you're probably wondering how ol' Pete is gonna manage all this," the man continued, rubbing his hands together. "Well, I'll tell ya. I got a buyer all lined up for the place in Chicago and movers ready to pack up and bring our stuff out. We can start house-huntin' tomorrow."

This was essentially true, Andrew reflected, although Pete was neglecting to mention that it was a done deal, whether his family liked it or not. And there was the little matter of employment.

As if Pete had read Andrew's mind, he continued. "And not only that, but I got a brand new career out here. Begins next month. Doesn't bring in as much as Locatelli Brothers"—Marti stiffened visibly—"but it's honest work for honest pay. Chief Ridley worked it all out for me."

Andrew now felt as blown away as everyone else in the room looked. Was this the same sorry-looking Pietro Locatelli who had been ready to turn himself in only thirty-six hours ago? "Uh . . . this sounds great, Pete," he managed, "but could you give it to us a little more slowly?"

"Sure, bishop," Pete said obligingly. "Lemme put it this way." He planted himself directly in front of his wife. "Marti, honey," he announced, "you are lookin' at a miracle. No more tobacco. No more workin' for Locatelli Brothers. No more Mr. Worthless slinkin' around the back alleys of Chicago." He hooked his thumbs proudly behind the edges of his shirt front. "Your Petey-sweetie's a genuine urban anthropologist." Beside Andrew, Jeanette drew a quick, audible breath. "He's gonna be the new gang-unit consultant for the regional law enforcement teams here in Utah. The chief just got the go-ahead from the commissioner. I'm on the good side of the law now, and I'm never lookin' back. How 'bout *that?*"

Marti sat silent for what seemed, in the still room, about half an hour, her face turning from white to red to purple and back again through a dozen different shades of each. She tried to speak about four times before she got out the strangled sentence, "Pete, if you're joking about any of this, I swear I'll hang you out to dry."

"Absolutely no joke. Phone the chief yourself and ask him. And then phone a real estate agent. But first, let's get that font filling."

Marti sat dumbstruck for another few moments. Then she gave a high-pitched giggle—or was it a hysterical sob? Then another. Then several together. She was laughing and crying at the same time.

Grasping Marti's hand, Pete swept her up from the recliner and into a huge bear hug. "Didn' I tell ya I'd take you places if you stuck with me, baby? Smoke-free today, baptized tomorrow, honestly employed next month, on to the temple in a year. Next stop, celestial kingdom!"

Like Andrew, everyone present knew that it wouldn't be that easy, but this was no time to quibble. This was a time for congratulations and rejoicing, and both flowed freely for several minutes. The only ones who seemed less than overjoyed were Vinnie and his family. In fact, it was Vinnie's daughter, Patrizia, who sounded the first plaintive note in the festivities. "But we'll be all alone back there," she complained. "And we have to go back to curfew at seven o'clock."

"For shame, Patz," her father reproved her. "Sure, Pete and Marti are leaving us in the lurch to defend ourselves against all those anti-Mormon aunts and uncles and prop up the ward all by ourselves, but this is their party."

Taking his cue from his father, Patz's brother, Michelangelo (Mick for short), added his own view. "Yeah, it'll be pretty dismal with our best friends and the only members in our family gone, but someone's got to be martyrs, I guess." He sighed dramatically.

This shadow on his perfect evening of triumph was more than Pete could bear. "Well, c'mon, Vinnie, what's holdin' you back there anyway? You're a computer whiz. You can get a job anywhere, ya know. Why hang around Chicago when you could be here?"

"Are you crazy, Pete? What about Cat? You think I can ask her to leave it all behind on a whim like this?" returned Vinnie with just a hint of heroic rhetoric to his tone. "She's got family, friends, a job, a home—how could I tell her to chuck it all?" He glanced sideways at his wife in an appraising manner, and

Andrew began to suspect that some sort of persuasion gambit was underway.

"Yeah, look at all we've got waiting for us in Chicago," Mick chipped in. "Curfew, gang action in the streets, hour-and-a-half bus ride to early-morning seminary every day, three girls in the whole ward to ask out . . ."

"Now just a minute, there are good things about Chicago, too," Cat protested. "The museums, the art galleries, the symphony, the lake, the universities . . ."

By now, Patz had picked up on her father's method. "The gunfire, the neighbors peddling drugs, the bars on every corner, the graffiti on every wall, half the girls at school pregnant . . ."

Abruptly Vinnie dropped the pretense. His loyalty to the ward in Chicago apparently extended only so far. "Sure, they've got good things in Chicago, Cat, but they've got them all here, too—not to mention quiet, safe neighborhoods, church steeples everywhere you look, mountains practically on your doorstep, and redrock deserts just a few hours away. The kids'll make friends who have standards like theirs. And how often does your family get together anyway? Wasn't it once in the past three years? Look, don't we spend most of our time at church and with Pete and Marti? Haven't you wanted a bigger place for the kids to grow in? And wouldn't you like to retire?"

Now Marti spoke up. "And if you don't stay, who's going to help Gina and me keep Pete on the strait and narrow?"

Cat wavered for a moment. "Mom'll have a fit," she protested weakly.

"Your mom spends three-quarters of her time in Vegas and Reno as it is," Vinnie pressed. "You're closer to her here than you were there."

Cat blinked meditatively. "I've always wondered what it would be like to live in a house with a yard." She paused, and her children nudged each other expectantly. "Oh, all right," she said crossly. She cut across the renewed cheering with a stern, "But I'm getting kind of old for all this change, folks."

Pete shot her a winning grin. "If I can change, anyone can, ya know? And don't worry about your family. If they give you a hard time, I'll just send the boys around to deal with them."

Marti scowled and cleared her throat dangerously. He turned toward her casually.

"Hey, I don't mean *those* boys," he specified, jerking a thumb toward the eastern wall of the living room. "I mean *these* boys." With a wave, he indicated the missionaries. "Look what their kind did for me."

Once the arrangements for Pete's baptism had been made and a date selected when Steve and Gina could attend Sister Jantzen at the temple, Andrew and Jeanette were free to leave with the missionaries for the short walk around the block to the Barlow home. The two young missionaries were, naturally, full of questions about Pete's apparently sudden conversion. Andrew filled them in with a few well-chosen sentences. Their curiosity satisfied, they strode ahead, exulting in the good fortune that had dropped an instant baptism into their laps and planning feverishly how to work the event into the impending discussion with the Ridleys. Andrew purposely lagged behind with Jeanette.

"An urban anthropologist," were her first words. "So Pete was the person Chief Ridley meant when he said that the guy didn't know what to call himself—and when he said that you were meeting someone with gangland connections at odd places late at night."

Now that the secret was out, Andrew saw no harm in sharing with her the whole story of Pete's place in the family business and that Saturday night beside the freeway overpass. By the end of it, Jeanette was giggling like a girl. "I'll bet Marti never envisioned Pete as a caped crusader fighting crime! No wonder she accused him of joking." Then she tucked her hand more securely into the crook of his elbow. "And no wonder you've been so distracted these past few days. That isn't your average ward problem. Next time I'll think twice before I decide that it must be my fault."

"Think more times than twice. It's never likely to be your fault," Andrew corrected her gently. "You've been more help to me than you realize."

"I don't see how," Jeanette began.

"Don't you? Isn't this the woman who saved my son's wedding to the girl of his dreams? The one who presented an adopted woman with her true blood heritage? The one who found a new livelihood for a destitute Slovenian family? The one who provided the clues the police needed to solve the mystery of their missing husband and father? The one who restored a reforming gangster's self-esteem by giving a name to his unique talents?" But there was no time to enlighten her further. The elders had mounted the Barlows' porch steps and rung the bell, and the senior Sister Barlow was opening the door to admit the party.

In the commotion that followed, as Tiffany—regally positioned on the couch amid cushions, crutches, and footstools—introduced the missionaries and made seating arrangements, Chief Ridley drew Andrew and Jeanette aside. "Before she micromanages my life away, I need to brief you about that grave robber."

Dead bodies again? What is it with this man? thought Andrew, putting a defensive arm around Jeanette. *And what's this business about robbing graves?*

"Mrs. McCammon, finding that gas worker was the greatest thing that could have happened. We called him down, and he identified the criminal right away. Then we called Mr. Jarvis, and he translated the guy's confession in full. We compared it to the widow's story and the detective's guesses, and I think we got a closed case."

Jeanette looked as perplexed as Andrew felt, but she said nothing.

"Seems the stiff got a good job and bought a car, then he phoned his family and told them to get ready to move to Vegas, that he'd be coming after them. Sent them some money, too. This ugly fella met him by chance and hitched a ride. Comes from Slo-whatever, same as they did, so it was only natural to help out another immigrant. Thing is, this guy's illegal and just got smuggled in. He says the stiff didn't know that. Well, they were cruisin' along I-15 down south, miles from anywhere, when Lenka's hubby took ill, pulled over, and died of a heart attack. Scared this illegal nigh to death. He stuffed the body into the trunk and kept driving, wonderin' what to do next.

"At first he was gonna abandon the car and the stiff in front of the family's house and run for it. He got the address from the guy's driver's license, and then he saw the wad of cash that was with it and got greedy. So when he got into town, he phoned the family and pretended to be Daddy. Told the family his car had broken down and to take the bus and meet him at the bus station in Vegas. Once they left the house, he buried the corpse."

Jeanette was incensed. "He was going to dump the body on their doorstep without any explanation? And then he decided to impersonate the man, leave them homeless and penniless, and let them dangle in suspense forever? That's heartless!"

"You're not kiddin'. Even Mr. Jarvis wouldn't offer a word in his defense. Only things that kept him from gettin' away with it entirely were the dog and that gas worker. Between them, they flustered him so bad that he dropped the stiff's wallet into the grave and didn't realize it till it was too late. Once he'd run through the cash, see, he decided to risk comin' back for the social security card and other ID. That's when the girls happened on him."

"What girls?" Andrew questioned. All this was new to him.

"Oh, Pete didn't tell you? My girl Bethany wanted to help the little Slo girl get through grieving for her dad, so they went to put flowers on his grave site. Walked right into the arms of the perp. Pete saw it happening from the treehouse in Roylances' yard and yelled at the goon to distract him. Between him yellin' and the girls screamin', they alerted Paddy and Justin, who were in the neighborhood. And the other dog—Laddie, I think they called him—came and brought his owner along for the ride. Made for one of the more exciting arrests we've had in this town. You oughta get Pete to tell you all about it."

"They got him? Thank goodness!" exclaimed Jeanette. "Are the girls all right?"

"Yep, 'cept that Bethy's grounded for a month for not tellin' her mom where they were going. I think I can talk Annabelle down to a week, though."

"And what about this grave robber?" Andrew asked.

"Well, we've got him for failure to report a death, desecration of a corpse, theft, driving without a license or insurance, telephone fraud, vandalism, car theft, attempted ID theft, and attempted aggravated assault. Once he's answered to all that, immigration wants him for illegal entry. Of course, we could make it easy and ask Granny Slo to come down to the station and kill him with a look."

Jeanette smiled at that. Andrew recalled the diminutive but feisty grandmother from his interview and agreed that she could probably do it. But he had another question.

"Pete just got finished telling us that you've found him a job."

"Sure did. May be the best hire I've ever made."

"But you knew about his background, didn't you?"

"'Course I did. We make a thorough background check of everyone we consider."

Andrew hesitated. He didn't want to ruin anything for Pete, but he didn't want Chief Ridley to take unnecessary chances with his own job. "For the record," he offered finally, "I personally feel that Pete will be an extremely loyal and diligent employee for you. And I'm willing to put it in writing for anyone who might think that his reformation is . . . uh . . . less than genuine."

"Oh, you mean if the commissioner thinks he's a mole for some crime boss? No problem there. Soon as I talked to him Monday evenin' and saw how guilty he was acting, I knew he was no mole. Moles've got to be better than that at playin' a part, see, or they don't stay undercover for long."

A sudden stillness in the room called Andrew, Jeanette, and Chief Ridley to attention. "Dad," Tiffany said sweetly, "Elder Tolliver just asked if he could give the opening prayer. Is that all right with you?"

"Yes, ma'am," the chief answered, moving hurriedly to join his wife on a front-row seat.

* * *

Jeanette hadn't been to a missionary discussion in quite some time. She was duly impressed by the fluent way in which the young men unfolded the gospel plan, seemingly unfazed by the chief's frequent drifts off topic. The entire Ridley family seemed very taken by the message. Rhett and his parents, too, seemed fascinated and rather awed, as if they were understanding certain points for the first time. The group had just collectively accepted an invitation to attend Pete's baptism on Saturday afternoon when Andrew tapped Jeanette's arm and motioned furtively toward the door. They departed quietly, waving a silent farewell to Tiffany.

"Unless I'm much mistaken, that young woman is going to carry her way with her whole family and her husband's," Jeanette commented as Andrew put the Beastie into gear and pulled away from the curb.

"I don't think you're mistaken at all," Andrew replied, "on this or very much else. But let's talk about them later. All day I've been wanting to tell you about someone really special."

"Who's that?"

"Her name is Jeanette McCammon."

The evening only improved as it went on. Jeanette had never even heard of Neville's and was delighted with it, intrigued with the architecture and décor, charmed by the medieval background music, and completely won over by the scrumptious napoléon pastries that were the specialty of the house. "This place is a gem! How did all the activities committees in my singles ward miss it for so many years?"

"I'm just glad that they did," Andrew confided. "because I wanted to take you to a place without any prior memories that might compete with tonight."

Jeanette stared at him. "R-really?" she stammered. "You've been worried about competing memories too?"

"Naturally. Just one look at you told me that you've probably had men following you around like lost puppy dogs for years."

She knitted her eyebrows. "Maybe a few," she conceded dubiously.

"No, those are just the ones you noticed at the time. I'll bet anything that plenty of others did, too—but they never got brave enough to make themselves known."

"But even the ones I knew about couldn't compare to you."

"That's what I want to hear. And it's my job to make sure that they never do." He leaned over the flaky, creamy remains of their napoléons and kissed her lightly. "Come on. We have another stop to make, and I think we've timed it just right."

Jeanette knew as soon as they arrived that the timing was ideal. A sunset with all the delicate tints of a ripe, blushing peach formed a stunning backdrop for a deep green arbor of the most fragrant roses she had ever smelled. The varicolored flowers and their foliage arched over a heavenly flagstone pathway that led westward to a rose-covered, eight-sided gazebo, equally enchanting, beside a river that seemed to flow directly out of Camelot. The entire scene was achingly, wondrously beautiful. Seated in the gazebo on a white, wrought-iron love seat with Andrew beside her, Jeanette inhaled the warm air heavy with the roses' perfume, certain that no fairy-tale princess could have been more adored. With his arm encircling her and her head against his shoulder, they sat with hands clasped and watched as the peach light faded to dusky rose and lilac behind the powder-blue clouds lining the horizon. The spell seemed unbreakable; she couldn't move or speak. She could only breathe in the sweetness and savor each perfect moment.

As the sunset colors deepened, Andrew lifted her hand to his lips and kissed it, lingeringly, passionately. "I didn't think I'd ever have the courage to come here again," he whispered as he pressed her palm against his cheek.

"Because of the memories?" she guessed.

"The memories and the loneliness. But with you here, I've got a past, a present, and a future again." His fingers stroked her hair, caressed her face. "You've given me back my life and the whole world. I can enjoy it, free from pain and longing. Lovely, darling Jeanette, never believe that you haven't done enough for me."

Five days ago, Jeanette could not have known what he meant. Now she understood.

CHAPTER 14
Epilogue in White

In contrast with their engagement, Mark and Alyssa's wedding transpired without a hitch. It was with a nearly equal blending of happiness and relief that Jeanette stood with Andrew, his children, their spouses, and Sister Dora Jantzen near the temple doors as they waited for the newlyweds to emerge.

Alyssa was stunningly beautiful in her wedding dress. Her smile was radiant and spontaneous every one of the four times that the photographer had her re-exit the temple in order to capture that "perfect" view of her veil streaming off into the breeze. Mark, on the other hand, looked joyful but somewhat dazed, as if he couldn't quite believe that she was his at last. Jeanette noted that he clung steadily to his bride's hand or kept an arm around her, as if that were the only way to keep her from being snatched from him again.

"He acts as if he's terrified that Bill Ross will show up and spirit her away," Andrew remarked to Jeanette in a low voice as the couple posed for a round of photos.

Eric heard him. "Bill Ross? That muscle-bound glamour-boy who tried so hard to impress Fio? He was after Alyssa too?"

His wife, Sheri, nudged him. "Bill's an okay guy for a girl who doesn't need an Einstein to make her happy. And at least he has good taste."

"Yeah, his choice of girls to chase was the most intelligent thing about him," Spencer observed, pulling Fiona closer to him, as if the unseen specter bothered him as well.

Kevin's wife, Heather, chuckled as she looked from Spencer back toward Mark. "Well, you can all set your minds at ease. Bill Ross is not at liberty to pursue women anymore."

"How would you know?" demanded Kevin, curiously but with a hint of suspicion.

Heather kissed him playfully. "No, he wasn't after me, too—he's too young. But his older sister was one of my best friends. I ran into her a few days ago while I was shopping for wedding gifts, and she says he's engaged."

"Engaged?" Andrew asked. "I didn't think he was home from his tour of duty yet."

"He isn't. He's temporarily posted in Hawaii, and on his first Sunday he went to sacrament meeting at a local ward with his servicemen's group. The next thing he knew, a Hawaiian couple had cut him off from his buddies, cornered him, and shoved a girl practically into his arms, saying, 'This is our daughter. Isn't she beautiful?' What could he say to that?"

"Mmmm," Eric mused. "That *is* a loaded question, under the circumstances."

"No kidding," Kevin concurred. "Polynesian girls *are* gorgeous—and some of their fathers are pretty buff."

"Well, Bill wasn't in any position to disagree, even with his wrestling skills to back him up. But since she really is beautiful—and he's obviously skilled at recognizing beautiful girls—they're getting married in the Hawaii Temple next month," Heather concluded, her eyes twinkling.

"Another happy ending," sighed Sister Jantzen, dabbing at her own eyes. Her sealing to her late husband had taken place two weeks previously, and she was evidently still glowing from that experience. She touched Jeanette's arm. "I'll be running along, dear. Thanks so much for inviting me. I'll see you this evening at the reception."

Almost at the same time, the photographer began motioning to them. "Let's get some shots of the groom's family."

Andrew patted Jeanette's hand in the crook of his arm as they moved toward the place the photographer was indicating in the temple gardens. After three other children's marriages and a previous one of his own, she guessed that he knew the routine by heart. But what he said surprised her. "I'm beginning to regret that we didn't do the whole professional photograph business and reception for you. It would have been your only chance—at least, I hope so."

Jeanette had to smile. *The man's a born romantic,* she thought tenderly. "I don't regret it," she assured him. "I'm not much for being in the spotlight. And I have what I wanted most."

"A home and family?"

"A wonderful husband, complete with good looks, brains, *and* spirituality. The home and family are icing on the wedding cake."

"Well, if you ever change your mind, I can arrange an anniversary party like no other, considering all the connections I've made."

"I'll bear that in mind."

* * *

Andrew had not the least occasion to regret his involvement in this wedding reception. Alyssa, who didn't care for formal reception lines, had instead opted for a line of photographs of the wedding party to be arranged on a long table, while the subjects of the photographs were instructed to circulate among the guests, relax, visit, and generally have a good time. "This is the way I like it," Jeanette whispered as they rose from a table to refresh their cups of punch. "Maximum freedom, minimum standing." Andrew agreed wholeheartedly.

"Hey, bishop!" The voice hailing him was familiar but unexpected.

Andrew turned to see Pete Locatelli moving toward them from the table where his wife and cousins, both Modonis and Roylances, were seated.

"Hello, Brother Locatelli. I didn't expect you back from Chicago so soon," Andrew said, extending his hand.

"Nothin' to keep us there once the house sale was closed," Pete replied in chipper tones, shaking Andrew's hand warmly with both of his. "And all that tobacco stench"—he paused to gag slightly—"was makin' me sick."

"Did Sister Locatelli forgive you when she found out that the house was sold before you came out here the first time?"

"Well, ya know," Pete answered a little more restrainedly, dropping the bishop's hand, "it didn't make sense to rile her up for no good reason. So I told the real estate agent to keep that out of the discussion. And until we signed the closing papers, the house really wasn't sold, ya know?"

"I see," Andrew said slowly.

"Anyway, now that we've got an address to ship the furniture to, it's on its way. And guess what? We'll be in your ward. We're buyin' that deserted house where the Slovenian guy was buried. The real estate agent gave us a bargain price on it—says he's had a bear of a time gettin' rid of it ever since the grave was discovered, ya know?"

"But that doesn't bother you?"

"Not in the least. If there was ever a ghost problem, I've laid it to rest. And it's perfect for us. Three bedrooms, two baths, just been fully remodeled by some lady that Chief Ridley calls Mrs. Airhead, and only a holler away from Gina's place."

Andrew supposed that nobody would know that better than Pete. "Is Sister Locatelli okay with it?"

"Sure, she is . . . well, actually,"—with an apologetic glance at Jeanette—"she doesn't exactly know about the grave in the backyard, ya know? I told the agent to keep quiet about it, that I'd break it to her later. So he said he guessed it was the garden. Somethin' *was* planted there, after all. And nobody's down there now."

"I see," Andrew answered even more slowly. *I see,* he told himself, *that I'm going to have to give a sacrament meeting talk about truly living the law of honesty.* Beside him, Jeanette stared steadily at the cultural hall floor, but he could sense from the very slight movements of her hand in his that she was on the verge of uncontrollable giggles.

"And guess what else? Vinnie and Cat are lookin' at houses in the ward too. They say they've got used to it here, ya know? Vinnie's got a job offer already. Hey, there's Chief Ridley now! Gotta talk to him—I start work next week!" And he was gone.

Jeanette collapsed against Andrew, shaking with suppressed laughter. He supported her with one arm and pressed the fingertips of his other hand to his forehead, which was beginning to throb with mild but distinct pain.

"Oh, Andrew!" Jeanette gasped when she could catch her breath. "You've definitely got your work cut out for you. It's a good thing that Gina's here to help you."

"Maybe," he replied dubiously. "But," he added with more assurance, "it's a lot better thing that you're here to help me." And he sealed the statement with a kiss.

About the Author

Elizabeth W. Watkins, the mother of two married children and a missionary and the grandmother of four girls, loves books, writing, music, and family history. Besides writing novels, she has enjoyed the opportunity to work on such research, writing, and publishing projects as the history of education in Zion, the associates of Joseph Smith, LDS history and doctrine, and the works of medieval philosophers. She lives in American Fork, Utah, with her husband and seven cats.